"S-sex?"

"Sex." Glory positioned her fingers at the sides of his mouth. "Say it with me, Sam. Sss...e...xxx. That's the physical expression of—"

"I *know* what it is, Glory. And you and I are not having it."

"But we have all the symptoms."

"For heaven's sake, Glory, sex isn't a treatable disease."

"Of course it's treatable. We just start kissing and—"

"You're from Mars, aren't you?"

"Don't be silly. Heaven is much closer than that."

Heaven was closer than he could handle at the moment. "It has to be that...or else, you're just plain crazy."

"You think I'm crazy because I want to have sex with you?"

"Look, Glory, in this day and age, I find it easier to believe you're from outer space than that you're a virgin."

She considered that with a slight frown. "I thought men liked virgins."

ABOUT THE AUTHOR

Karen Toller Whittenburg lives in the beautiful green countryside of northeastern Oklahoma. Her favorite pastime hasn't changed since she was a child—curling up with a good book. She divides her leisure time between family activities and writing movie scripts for the Narrative Television Network, a network for the blind and visually impaired. Karen and her husband love to spend weekends browsing through antique shops. He collects old cameras and she collects ideas for future books.

Books by Karen Toller Whittenburg

HARLEQUIN AMERICAN ROMANCE

197—SUMMER CHARADE
249—A MATCHED SET
294—PEPPERMINT KISSES
356—HAPPY MEDIUM
375—DAY DREAMER
400—A PERFECT PAIR
424—FOR THE FUN OF IT
475—BACHELOR FATHER
528—WEDDING OF HER DREAMS
552—THE PAUPER AND THE PRINCESS

HARLEQUIN TEMPTATION

303—ONLY YESTERDAY

Karen Toller Whittenburg

NANNY ANGEL

Harlequin Books

TORONTO • NEW YORK • LONDON
AMSTERDAM • PARIS • SYDNEY • HAMBURG
STOCKHOLM • ATHENS • TOKYO • MILAN
MADRID • WARSAW • BUDAPEST • AUCKLAND

For all my guardian angels:
Mom and Dad,
Jill,
Debbi and Crystal, the birthday angels,
and, as always,
Don

ISBN 0-373-16572-2

NANNY ANGEL

Copyright © 1995 Karen Toller Whittenburg.

Printed in U.S.A.

Chapter One

With the floppy body of her favorite toy dragon tucked firmly against her side, Allison Jill Oliver tip-toed from her bedroom to the top of the stairs. She lifted the hem of her nightgown and paused, poised like a ballerina on point, before quietly scampering down to the landing. There, she hovered in the shadows, as still as a mouse, waiting and listening, before she edged across to peer through the wooden balusters and down at the hallway below. "Ssshhhh, Hunny," she whispered to the stuffed toy. "Don't make any noise or he'll send us back to bed."

The bedraggled dragon was obediently quiet and Allie hugged his scrawny neck even tighter as she studied the partially opened door of Sam's office. He was in there—when he was home, he was always in there—and she wanted to go in and sit on his lap and ask him to read her a story. But Sam didn't like to be int'rupted. And he didn't like to read to her. He would just say that she was five years old now and old enough to understand that he had *work* to do and that she should *act* like a big girl and *stay in bed* and *go to sleep,* like he'd told her *not five minutes ago.*

Allison sighed and sat down on her bottom. She slid her bare feet through the open spaces between the balusters and let her legs dangle over the edge of the stairwell. She didn't feel like going to dumb old sleep. She wanted to hear *The Best Nest.* It was her favorite book and she hadn't heard it since Sam had brought her home from Grandmother's. Sam said she knew all the words, anyway, and could read it to herself. But she didn't really know the words. She just 'membered what page they were on. 'Cept for when she got mixed up.

Grandmother said that ever'body got mixed up sometimes. Even Sam. But Grandmother liked *The Best Nest* almost as much as Allie did, and Sam didn't like *any* stories. Allie didn't think he liked her, either, even if Grandmother said he did.

"If I could have reached you during normal business hours, I wouldn't be calling at this time of the night." Impatience crackled in the voice that carried all the way from the study up to the stair landing.

Allison wrapped her fingers around one of the stair posts and pressed her face against the wood.

"Yes, it's an emergency!" Sam's voice continued. "I have a meeting at eight in the morning and I need you to send another nanny for my daughter. Immediately." He paused, then raised his voice again. "Look, I did *not* dismiss Mrs. Maggard. She left ... without notice, I might add.... I beg your pardon? Now, how the hell could it be *my* fault...? Well, of course I realize Allie can be difficult at times.... Yes, I suppose spending the past year with her grandparents may have spoiled her a little, but she's barely five years old. How could she have alienated an experienced nanny like Mrs. Maggard in a matter of less than a week?"

Allison puckered her mouth in a frown. She hadn't meant to aleeate anybody, but she was glad Mrs. Maggard was gone. She hadn't been very nice and she had a big nose and teeth that made little clicks like the clock on Sam's desk, and she made cheese sandwiches for lunch. Every day. And she never fixed applesauce for Hunny.

"I am not going to argue with you," Sam said in the same voice he had used when he'd stepped on the spaghetti Allie hadn't eaten after all. "I do understand your position, Mrs. Klepperson, but you must have someone who can come on short notice. Your advertisement clearly states that—and this is a direct quote—'the Guardian Angel Nanny Service can meet any emergency. Our angels go anywhere, anytime.' Now, will you find someone for me, or do I need to call another agency?"

Allison sucked on her bottom lip and let her feet swing back and forth, back and forth.

"I see. Well, that is certainly your prerogative, Mrs. Klepperson, but in the interest of goodwill and the continued success of your business, I strongly suggest you rethink your— Damn!" The phone receiver clattered in its cradle and the noise was followed by a gruff and angry rumble of words.

Allie clapped her hands over the dragon's ears. "Don't listen, Hunny. Sam isn't mad at you. He knows it's not your fault Mrs. Maggard left and now he has to get another *garden* angel." She stroked Hunny's soft, lumpy head. "If Mommy lived here instead of Heaven, Sam wouldn't be mad all the time and he wouldn't have to do so many works and he would read *The Best Nest* to us every night."

Music came on inside the office and Allison sighed with heartfelt frustration. "He's listening to *the song,*" she whispered. "Now he'll be mad *and* sad." Grandmother had told her that the music made Sam 'member her mother, but Allie didn't like *the song*. She didn't 'member her mother. And sometimes she got afraid that Sam would go away again and never come back, and she might not 'member him, either.

She heard the silvery clink of glass against glass and knew he was getting a drink. She squeezed her eyes shut, wishing and wishing that she was in Sam's office right now. Once, a long time ago, he'd let her sleep on the sofa while he did work at his desk, and when she'd woken up, he'd given her a glass of orange juice and told her a story about a littlest angel. He'd even said the angel had a pet dragon, just so Hunny would feel 'cluded. But after Mommy got dead, Allie had asked him to tell the story again and he'd said he didn't know any stories about angels. Hunny had cried and cried like a big baby and wouldn't go to sleep. Allison had had to sing his "Puff" song, even though she didn't know all the words, and Hunny kept crying and crying all night, anyway.

Allie took hold of the dragon's front feet and plopped the toy in her lap. With steely determination, she grabbed the scraggly whiskers on his chin and forced him to look at her with his pop-button black eyes. "Don't you start crying, Hunny," she admonished in a stern whisper. "'Cause I'm not singing 'Puff' to you. You're all grown up and you have to stop acting like a baby. And if you keep causin' problems, Sam might send you away and there'd be nobody to give you applesauce. So you have to be good from now on, just like the Littlest Angel's dragon." She gave the toy a shake for emphasis. "Do you hear me?"

Hunny pouted, as she'd known he would, so she hugged him tight against her flannel nightgown and told him he was the very best dragon in the whole wide world and she loved him very much and that she'd think of some way to keep Sam from being mad because Mrs. Maggard left and he had to get another garden angel to take care of them.

The idea was so unexpected, so perfectly wonderful, that Allie had to stop and admire it for a minute before she could confide it into Hunny's trusting ears. "We can get the angel for Sam," she whispered. "Then he'll be happy and...and...he'll read us a story." Just the thought of it made her feel good.

But how was she going to get an angel? That part of the story she couldn't 'member. Allie studied the problem for several minutes before she sighed and pulled herself up from the stair step. "We'll have to ask Sam," she said.

Hunny didn't want to, but Allison grabbed him by the tail and dragged him behind her as she padded down the remaining steps and quietly approached the study door. She hesitated, then gave the door a little push. It swung inward with a telltale squeak, but Sam didn't seem to hear. He was leaning back in his big black chair, listening to *the song*.

Hunny trembled in her hand and Allie wanted to run upstairs as fast as she could and jump under the covers before Sam saw her and got mad. But if she did that, she might never find out how to get an angel. She pulled the dragon into her arms and took two baby steps into the room.

"Sam?" she said as soft as a mouse's ear, bracing herself for his reply. When he still didn't look her way, she gulped and said it again, a little louder. "Sam?"

He lifted his head. "Allison! What are you doing out of bed? Didn't I tell you what was going to happen if you got up again?"

His voice made her skin feel all rough and itchy and she just stared at him as she clutched Hunny protectively to her chest.

"What is it this time?" he asked. "Another drink?"

She shook her head in emphatic silence and stood rooted to the floor.

The big chair made a gloomy creak as he leaned forward. "Allie," he said in a soft voice she didn't like any better than the loud one, "why aren't you in bed?"

She took a deep breath and blurted out her question. "Where do angels live?"

"Oh, Allie, not tonight." He took off his reading glasses, laid them on the desktop, and rubbed his eyes. "Why couldn't you just go to sleep, like I asked?"

She wanted to tell him that she couldn't go to sleep without a bedtime story, that she was afraid he might go away again if she closed her eyes too tight. But Sam didn't like her to say things like that and she didn't want to make him any madder. She knew it wasn't fair, but she shoved Hunny into the line of fire. "Hunny wanted applesauce," she said in quickly calculated self-defense.

"Allison." Suddenly his voice sounded as tired as Ethel's, the dog next door. Once in a while, from behind her fence, Ethel would let out a low, slow "wwwooooff," like she didn't have the energy to work up a real bark. With a shake of his head, Sam pushed up from the desk and walked around the edge.

Allison stood her ground, but she kept Hunny between her and her father. "He said his stomach hurt. And he wouldn't let me go to sleep."

Sam reached the doorway and, in one swift maneuver, scooped up daughter and dragon. "If Hunny eats any more applesauce, he's going to be so fat I won't be able to carry him upstairs to bed."

His voice suddenly didn't sound mad anymore, and Allie clamped her arms around his neck, letting Hunny snuggle his nose into Sam's shirt collar. "Let us stay in here with you, Sam," she asked. "I promise I'll make Hunny be real, real, rreaalll quiet."

Sam paused at the foot of the stairs and shifted her in his arms. "Dragons are never quiet unless they're asleep."

"Then I'll make Hunny go to bed and I'll stay with you. Pleeesse, Sam?"

His sigh was long and deep. "Allison, how many times do I have to explain? I have work to do. You have to stop popping out of bed every few minutes with some silly excuse to get my attention."

"But Hunny—"

"Hunny will stay in bed if you do. This is the third time tonight I've had to tuck you in and it will be the last time. Do you understand?"

Allie pouted as Sam carried her upstairs to her bedroom, but he didn't seem to care. He didn't look too happy, either, as he tucked the covers around her, and she knew there was no use asking him to read *The Best Nest*. "Sam?" she said to keep him from leaving right away. "I have to know about the angels. It's 'portant."

"I've told you, Allie, your mother went to live with the angels and—"

"No," Allie interrupted. "I have to know where they live and how I can talk to them."

He brushed her forehead with his hand and the sad look in his eyes got sadder. "Angels are like the stars in the sky. They can hear you no matter where you are when you talk to them. You don't even have to close your eyes or say the words aloud. Your guardian angels are always with you, Allie. They keep you safe and take care of you when I'm not around to do it."

"That's what you need, isn't it, Sam? A garden angel."

He straightened with a sigh. "Yes, Allie, that is exactly what I need. Now, go to sleep. We'll talk about this some other time."

"Sam?"

His quick frown was daunting. "Allison, do you remember that talk we had about how it was rude for you to call me Sam instead of Dad?"

"But Grandmother calls you Sam. And Grandma Lu calls you Sam. And Grandpa Gene calls you Sam. And Damon calls you Sam. And your secretary calls you Sam. And when you answer the phone you always say—" Allie lowered her voice "—Sam Oliver."

"That's true, Allison, but I'm your father and you shouldn't call me that."

"Hunny calls his father Big Bert and that isn't rude."

"But that's..." He shut his eyes and Allie wondered if he had gotten sleepy all of a sudden. But then he opened them again and she saw the sad was still inside. "Never mind, Allison. Just *please* go to sleep."

"Okay, Sam." She snuggled the covers under her chin. "I'll go right to sleep. And Hunny will, too. I promise we will."

He nodded and turned away.

"Sam?"

It took a minute, but he finally turned back around. "What is it, Allie?"

"I'm sorry I got out of bed after you tol' me not to for the third time."

He laid his hand on her forehead as he bent down to kiss her cheek. "I'm sorry, too, Allie."

She didn't know what he was sorry for, but she wished he wouldn't listen to *the song* anymore. She watched as he walked to the bedroom door. "Sam?"

He sighed and turned again, hand on the doorknob.

"Hunny wants you to leave the hall light on, 'kay?"

"Okay, but I want Hunny to stay under those covers until morning...no matter how hungry he gets. You tell him I said so." Sam positioned the door so that the light from the hallway made an illuminating strip across the floor. "Now, for the last time, good night."

"I won't let Hunny get out of bed anymore, Sam. I promise. I'll make him be quiet and go to sleep and—"

"*Good night,* Allison."

"Good night, Sam." The moment she heard his footsteps on the stairs, Allie scrambled out of bed, being careful to keep Hunny under the covers. She leaned down to give the dragon a kiss on his fuzzy nose. "You go right to sleep, Hunny, and maybe the angel will bring you some applesauce when she comes, 'kay?"

The dragon seemed content with that and Allison tiptoed to the window. She rested her elbows on the wooden sill, propped her hands under her chin, and looked up at the twinkling stars. "Is anybody out there?" she whispered.

There was a small sound outside. A quiet sound, like the rustle of angel wings, and Allie plunged on with her request. "Sam needs a garden angel," she said in a rush. "Tonight. It's very 'portant. Please send one right away."

Nothing happened, but Allie watched the stars expectantly, wondering how long it took to get from Heaven to Oklahoma. She wanted to keep watch for the angel, but her toes felt cold and she didn't want Sam to catch her out of bed again. With one last, long look at the sky, she turned away from the window and scampered across the room. Just as she reached the bed, she spun around and raced back to the window, pressing her nose and her palms against the cool glass pane.

"I 'most forgot," she said. "Thank you. Thank you very much." Then, quick as a bunny, she ran and jumped into bed, snuggled a drowsy Hunny in her arms, and smiled her way into sleep.

Chapter Two

Sam opened the French doors and stepped from his study into Jenny's rose garden. Not that it was much of a garden anymore. None of the rosebushes had survived. But then how could they have, without Jenny? They were nothing now but dead branches, all thorns and no promise. If he were the slightest bit brave, he would dig them up by the roots and put them out of their misery. But he couldn't bring himself to destroy the last remnant of Jenny's garden.

He shoved his hands into his trouser pockets and rattled the coins and keys he kept there. A nervous habit he noticed more and more frequently. That, and snapping at his daughter every time she came within ten feet of him. The coins and keys jangled again. He forced his hands out of his pockets, folded his arms across his chest, and tried not to think about the lousy job he'd done in his first week as a full-time father.

The air around him was crystal clear, sweetened with the scent of early spring, laced with the leftover chill of winter. Overhead, stars blinked and shimmered like distant campfires and the moon was little more than a shiny quarter slot in the deep, dark sky. There was something unusual about the evening, he thought. A restlessness, a certain ethereal sort of energy traveling with the breeze.

His hands slipped back into his pockets. It would probably rain like hell tomorrow. He turned on his heel and walked back inside, shutting the doors behind him, closing out the possibility that he deserved anything more than a lifetime of rainy days.

As he fastened the security latch, a quicksilver curve of light reflected in the glass panels of the door, and he glanced up in time to see the last glimmer of a shooting star on its final arc through the galaxy. With the accurate, deadly aim of a tender moment, Jenny's voice echoed in his memory. *Shooting star, count to three, make a wish for me and thee.*

He stepped back abruptly and closed the blinds. What was he looking at? Shooting stars were for lovers. Not for him. Not anymore. In a matter of minutes he was back at his desk and absorbed in his work.

Clank! Clatter! Crash!

The noise came from outside on the back patio, and Sam slapped his pencil onto the desk. "Ethel," he said tightly. He tossed his glasses onto the blueprints, pushed back his chair, and headed for the back of the house, ready to do battle. That damn basset hound must have gotten out of her yard again and was scavenging the neighborhood trash cans, scattering garbage from one end of the block to the other—an adventure she had waddled through twice this week already.

Sam did not understand why people who insisted on having pets couldn't keep them chained up and off other people's property. This time, he decided, Ethel could damn well spend a day or two in the city dog pound for her trouble, and her owners could damn well spend the money to bail her out. Maybe then they'd keep her away from his trash.

Still grumbling, he crossed the kitchen and switched on the back porch light, looking out through the back door window and grimacing at the mess already strewn across the patio. An empty tuna can rolled in a smooth circle, finally coming to rest upside down at the edge of the lawn. Only one of the four aluminum trash containers remained upright, but it rocked ominously half in, half out of the shadows at the side of the patio.

Sam jerked open the door. "Get out of there, you stupid mutt, before I break all four of those stubs you call legs!"

The trash container stopped wobbling. "Couldn't you just help me up?" The voice that came out of the darkness was light and lyrical, female and friendly.

"Ethel?" Sam said, and then felt stupid. The neighbor's basset hound wasn't smart enough to bark, much less speak English. "Who's out there?" he asked gruffly to cover his gaffe. "And what are you doing in my trash?"

"I'm sitting in it." A thread of laughter wove through the words. "You know, Sam, this is a little embarrassing. Could you give me a hand?"

She had called him by name, but her voice, while pleasant, was unfamiliar. Suppose this was an elaborate ruse to burglarize the house? There were any number of papers in those trash containers that identified him by name. Was he about to step outside and meet the business end of a sawed-off shotgun?

Her laughter caught him by surprise and made him smile, even though he couldn't think of a single reason he had for smiling.

"You're a suspicious human, aren't you?" the voice asked. "All right, let me try this one more time...." Five slender fingers curved over the rim of the lone, standing trash container.

Sam thought he should probably shut the door, bolt the locks, and call the police instead of waiting for a shotgun to appear. But he couldn't seem to get his feet moving.

"Feet are quite a nuisance, I'm discovering. I'm not sure I'll ever get used to them." Five fingers became ten and he could see they were attached to a pair of smooth hands, which extended into a pair of shapely arms and ...

His jaw dropped as the intruder rose from the shadows and into the halo of the porch light. She was blond, a glow of riotous curls covering her head—the only part of her extraordinary body that *was* covered. Her skin fairly gleamed with a virginal blush, and when Sam tried to catch his breath, the air wheezed past his Adam's apple as if it were a worn-out bellows.

"Are you in pain?" she asked.

His chest hurt. His throat was tight. His whole body was becoming decidedly uncomfortable, but he wouldn't exactly describe the sensations as painful. It had been a long time since he'd seen a naked woman and never, in his entire life, had he seen one who looked like this. "Who...? What...are you doing?"

She looked down at the hands she had clamped securely on the rim of the trash container. "Getting acquainted with gravity, I think."

"Gravity," he repeated as he tried to gather his scattered thoughts. "But...what are you doing *here*?"

Her chin came up, bringing her startled blue eyes to meet his. "Allison invited me." She made it sound as if Allison had invited her to a birthday party, as if she were surprised that he would even ask.

He rubbed the pad of his thumb along his jaw and tried to keep his gaze from straying below her neck. "And...how do you know Allison?"

The woman laughed in instant delight. "Oh, everyone knows Allison."

That was hardly reassuring, and then a rather daunting connection struck him. "You're not, by any chance, from the Guardian Angel agency, are you?"

Her cupid's bow mouth dipped into a reluctant frown. "Well, *technically,* I'm only an apprentice angel."

So, Mrs. Klepperson had sent someone after all, Sam thought. An apprentice nanny. A trainee. And a naked one, at that. "Tell me, Miss Apprentice, when you become a full-fledged angel, will you be expected to wear clothes?"

"Clothes!" She gave a funny little gasp and looked down. "Oh, no! I knew I'd forget something." Her bare shoulder lifted in a shrug. "The other angels call me the go-getter, because I'm always having to go back and get something I forgot."

Sam sighed. In his experience, any woman who was this cheerful while that naked wasn't high on anything as harmless as moonlight. "So, why don't you do that now?" he suggested.

"Do what?"

"Go back to wherever you came from and get the clothes you forgot."

"Oh, I never had any clothes to begin with." She laughed, another throaty, pleasing sound. "You're my first assignment."

"No kidding."

"Really, you are. And I was so excited, I guess I didn't listen carefully to all the steps Leonard told me to follow."

"Leonard," Sam repeated, thinking he might have been too quick to abandon his theory of a burglary attempt. Her accomplice might be picking the lock on the front door at this very moment. "You may be surprised to learn that I have a Bulldog alarm system. State of the art. One flip of the switch and the whole police department will be here before you can say 'Hand over your valuables.'" He snapped his fingers to demonstrate and then wondered what in the hell he was doing.

"Why would I say that?" She lifted one finger from the aluminum rim and then tentatively raised another. "And what would I do with your...what did you call them?"

"Valuables," he snapped. "And you'd sell them, that's what you'd do."

"Who to?"

"Some fence, probably."

She looked up and giggled. "A fence?" she asked. "Really?"

He was going inside. Right now. But for some reason he stood rooted in the doorway, staring at her as she took a small step to the side, swayed a little, and grabbed the rim of the trash can again for balance.

"Walking isn't as easy as I thought it would be," she said, and tried again, this time bringing her whole body, from bare toes to bare head, into the muted pool of the patio light.

Sam could no longer resist the wayward impulse that drove his attention to the supple flare of her waist, the slender curve of hips that led down into long, long legs. His throat tightened again and a swirl of anxious excitement knotted in his stomach. This was a dream. He'd fallen asleep at his desk and he was dreaming . . . and doing a magnificent job of it, too.

She wobbled and threw her arms out for balance, as if she were perched on a tightrope, forty feet up. "You know, Sam, it wouldn't hurt you to help me inside," she said.

Wait a minute. He wasn't dreaming. He could feel the nip of the March breeze. He could hear the basset hound snuffling along the perimeter of the fence that separated his house from the neighbors'. And he could damn well see the beautiful and very immodest woman who was weaving unsteadily across his patio. What difference did it make if she were a prospective burglar or the nanny he'd requested? She was not getting inside his house.

"You can't come in here," he said, hoping against hope that Allie wouldn't make another trip downstairs and, consequently, learn more about anatomy than any five-year-old needed to know. "You'll just have to leave."

"Oh, don't worry." The smile on her lips nearly beamed with reassurance. "Allie is sound asleep. There won't be anymore applesauce runs tonight."

Sam blinked. From now on, he was going to pay more attention to the kind of information he put in the trash. "Now, look, I don't know who you are, but—"

"I'm Glory," she said. "I'm your guardian angel."

"No. No, you're not." He shook his head. "I'm sorry, but I need someone with more experience...and clothes." With that, he shut the door, closing it with force and finality. Mrs. Klepperson was about to receive another after-hours phone call, he decided. What kind of sicko was the woman, anyway? Sending a nymphette like that to take care of a five-year-old child. Sam snapped the dead bolt, switched off the porch light, and resisted the impulse to peek through the back window to see if the blonde was still out there.

And what if she was?

He probably should call the police, either way. A woman like that, roaming the streets.... The doorbell chimed the first two bars of the "Hallelujah Chorus" and Sam jumped, startled. Now who the hell could that be?

Before he had time to think of the possibilities, the chimes rang again, loud and clear, and Sam hurried toward it. The truth was, he'd rather face almost anyone—from naked nanny to prospective burglar—than have another bedtime go-round with Allison tonight. As it was, he figured he'd be lucky if she didn't reach the door before he did.

Thankfully, there was no sign, or sound, of Allie as he moved past the stairs and through the entry hall. He grabbed the doorknob and paused just long enough to allow himself a peek through one of the foyer's narrow windows. The woman on his front porch was facing away from the door and all he could see was the very proper lines of her navy blue suit and the stern, silver clip clamped across the wayward blond curls at her nape.

The "Hallelujah Chorus" reverberated around him and he jerked open the door.

"Hello, again." Her smile nearly knocked him off his feet. "I got the clothes."

Sam's throat went dry as his grip on the doorknob intensified.

She did a wobbly, off balance pirouette for his inspection and faced him again, all smiles and obviously delighted with herself. "You're never going to believe where I found these."

He closed his eyes and then opened them for a second look. She could not be standing here on his front porch, fully clothed, when only moments before....

"I got the whole outfit right out of that *Architectural Digest* magazine you threw away. Even the hairstyle." Her fingers fluffed the wispy curls that framed her face. "Actually, I picked out the leather pants and jacket in the Harley-Davidson motorcycle ad, but Leonard said this would be more appropriate. What do you think?"

He thought he was hallucinating. "How...? How did you...do that?"

Her eyebrows pulled together in brief consideration. "Well, I had to have a little help. Leonard has more experience getting dressed than I do."

Sam shook his head. "But there wasn't...you didn't...have time."

She laughed and leaned forward to press the doorbell again, cocking her head to listen as the lush notes chimed through the house. "I *love* that song." She moved right past him and into the foyer. "Oh, look at these..."

Before Sam could catch his breath, she was at the foot of the stairs, admiring the portraits that lined the wall. "You have pictures of Allison," she said as if the camera had witnessed a miracle in every exposure. "There she is on her first birthday. Oh, and there the two of you are together with Jenny. And there's Janice...and Jim, Jenny's parents. Oh, and your parents, Lu and Gene. And you and Jenny at your college graduation. And here's another picture of Allie as a baby and one when she was three. What a precious child." With a shake of blond curls, she switched her sunny smile back on him. "I'm so happy you have these pictures."

Sam had never considered that all of the detailed information and family history he'd given the Guardian Angel Nanny Service might come back to haunt him. He'd actually thought the endlessly detailed forms he'd completed were for his and Allison's protection. He stepped away from the door, his own protective instincts rising to the fore. "Listen, you can't barge in here and—"

"Oh, look at that!" And she disappeared into his study.

"Just make yourself at home," he finished lamely. With a frown, he took a moment to close the front door and then walked to the doorway of his study. She was standing behind his desk, holding his glasses up to the overhead light, and he wondered if he should try a slide tackle across the desk or wait until she tried to get past him and grab her then.

Like a child with a new toy, she turned the glasses in every direction before finally setting them, crookedly, on the tip of her nose. "What do you do with these?" She squinted through the prescription lenses. "They make everything fuzzy," she observed.

Positioning his body squarely in the doorway, he placed a hand on either side of the casing. Let her get past him this time, he thought. "Those are my reading glasses."

She frowned at him over the tortoiseshell frames. "You don't read."

"Of course, I read."

"Allison says you don't." She pulled off the glasses and dropped them onto the desk. "What are these?" she asked, her attention diverting to the notes he had scattered precisely and laboriously across the blueprints.

"Don't touch those...." But Sam couldn't move fast enough to save the papers already sifting through her fingers and drifting like drowsy snowflakes to the floor.

She laughed and grabbed for the last lazy page, which fluttered up and then settled, like a free-floating feather, at Sam's feet.

He lifted his gaze from the paper to her. "I think you'd better give me your badge number before you cause any more trouble."

"I don't have a badge," she said. "But I suppose I could show you my halo registration."

He acknowledged her little joke with a humorless smile. "I think your name will suffice."

She nodded agreeably and turned to look at the bookshelves behind his desk. "If you don't read, what do you do with all these books?"

Sam's jaw began to ache. "I thought you were going to tell me your name."

"I thought I already did." She smiled in the face of his murderous glare. "I'm Glory."

"Glory what?"

"Glory *what?*"

Sam took a deep breath and spoke slowly and distinctly. "*What* comes after Glory?"

"Hallelujah?"

"All right, that's it. I don't know who you are or who put you up to this, but the joke is over. You've had your fun and now I want you out of my study and out of my house."

"No!" Allison's voice came from the direction of the doorway, high-pitched and indignant. "She's the garden angel, Sam! You can't send her away!"

He turned to meet his daughter's determined stare. "Allison," he said tightly. "I thought we agreed that you wouldn't get out of bed again tonight."

"Hunny wanted to see the angel." Allie lifted her chin. "And the doorbell rang."

"That is no excuse. Now, you march right back upstairs and take that mangy dragon with you."

"Hunny isn't mangy!" She stomped her foot and hugged the toy against her chest. "He's the best dragon in the whole world and you should 'pologize for calling him names."

"Don't be ridiculous, Allison. I am not apologizing to a stuffed toy."

Tears welled up in Allie's brown eyes. "Now look what you've done, Sam. You made him cry!"

A familiar frustration rose in Sam's chest. He didn't know how to be a father. Hell, he didn't even know how to talk to a moth-eaten toy dragon. "Go upstairs and get into bed, Allison. Right now."

Chin up, shoulders back, she stood her ground like David against Goliath. "Allison..." Sam warned her. "Don't make me come over there and..."

The soft, soothing sounds of an old folk song rolled over his shoulder, and Sam glanced back at Glory. She was singing Hunny's favorite tune as she moved from behind the desk and stooped to Allison's level, not too close to the child, but approachable.

Allie's defiance transformed into wonder. And as the song continued, she began to sing, too. Just a note. Two or three lyrics here and there. Her reedy voice adding a sweet and random harmony to Glory's throaty tones.

Sam watched in helpless and inhibited dismay as his daughter, her face lit up like a Fourth of July sparkler, walked right past him to stand, wide-eyed and receptive, before the stranger. She held out the dragon, offering his motley green head for the touch of Glory's hand, and Sam's heart grew heavy with envy. Why couldn't he have consoled the dragon and, consequently, his daughter? Why hadn't he thought to stoop to Allie's level instead of demanding that she adhere to his? Even a lost soul like Glory knew how to deal with his daughter, he thought. Everyone seemed to know. Everyone, except him.

"We were waiting for you," Allison said when the last lyrics had been sung. "This is Hunny. He likes applesauce and 'Puff' is his favorite song."

Glory smiled. "I thought it might be. 'Puff' is a beautiful song," she said. "My name is Glory and I like applesauce, too."

Allie cocked her head. "Do you like cheese sandwiches?"

"I think pizza is better."

"So do I."

And just like that, the deed was done, Sam thought. His daughter was under the spell of this latest, and unexpected, offering from the Guardian Angel Nanny Service.

"Allison, go upstairs." His voice was a gruff intrusion, an implacable authority that brought an abrupt halt to the magic.

Allie's lower lip trembled as she turned to face him. "I don't want to."

He tried to caution her with a lift of his brow.

She squared her shoulders—and stood her ground. "You'll send Glory away."

An undeniable charge, one that he wasn't fool enough to open for discussion. "Don't argue with me, Allie. I'll take you upstairs and put you into bed if I have to, but I'm asking you to be a big girl and do as you're told."

Her lower lip jutted forward in a stubborn pout. "I'm not a big girl. I'm little. And I'm not going to bed."

Glare for glare, he matched her challenge with fatherly omnipotence—until she swung the dragon up and into her arms as if the ragtag toy were her talisman against evil and headstrong fathers. At that moment Sam knew he didn't have a prayer of getting Allison upstairs and into bed without an avalanche of tears and a mountain of ugly threats.

"Did you see that?" Glory's awed whisper sliced the standoff down the middle. "Did you see Hunny yawn?"

Allison's whole attention diverted to the toy in her arms. "He's not yawning," she told Glory. "See?"

Glory pressed her lips in a slight frown. "I must have imagined . . . no, look, he's doing it again. He is yawning, isn't he, Sam?"

Sam couldn't see anything but a dingy smirk on the dragon's mouth, but he nodded in solemn agreement.

"Yes, I can see all the way to his tonsils. He must be very, very sleepy."

Allison took the dragon by his whiskers, turned him around, and studied him before she raised her doubt to Sam. "I don't think dragons have tompsulls."

Sam was willing to concede the point. "Maybe I was wrong about that. But I know for sure that dragons like to get lots of sleep."

Suspicion darkened her big brown eyes. "Hunny doesn't."

"Then he's an unusual dragon," Glory said with a knowledgeable smile. "Because when dragons sleep, they dream about wonderful things like applesauce and angels and little girls named Allison."

Allie considered the possibility and Sam considered the very lovely, very perceptive young woman who had literally dropped into his evening. She looked as wholesome as popcorn in her pin-striped Mary Poppins suit. Innocence was starched right into the tucks in her prim white blouse. If he hadn't seen her naked not ten minutes ago, he might have believed she was the answer to his prayers. On the other hand, if he hadn't seen her naked not ten minutes ago, he wouldn't be standing here now wondering if he'd been praying for the wrong thing all along.

"Does Hunny dream about me?" Allison's question jerked his thoughts back onto the straight and narrow.

"Every chance he gets," Glory said as if she knew. "Do you think Hunny could stop yawning long enough to hear a bedtime story before he falls asleep?''

"*The Best Nest?*" Allie displayed a judicious interest. "That's his favwrit."

"Oh, that's a wonderful story. Why don't you go upstairs now and get into bed? Your daddy will be up in a few minutes to read *The Best Nest* to you and Hunny. Would you like that?''

Allie's shoulders drooped. "Sam doesn't read."

"But I saw his reading glasses." Glory then indicated the overflowing bookshelves. "And he has all these books."

"He doesn't read *The Best Nest.*"

"That's not fair, Allison." Sam felt obliged to defend himself. "I've read that book to you dozens of times."

"When?"

She didn't remember, he realized with a start. She really didn't remember. "I'll read it tonight, Allie. I'll come upstairs and read *The Best Nest,* just as soon as I've finished my business with Miss...uh, with Glory."

The dragon slid to a neutral position at her side as Allie weighed her options. "You won't make her go away, will you? Hunny and I like her better than Mrs. Maggard."

"I know." Sam touched Allie's fine, dusty blond hair, then put his hands on her shoulders and pointed her toward the doorway.

"Good night, Allison," Glory said. "Good night, Hunny."

"I'll see you tomorrow, 'kay, Glory? You'll be here when I wake up, 'kay? And we'll . . . we'll play and . . . and sing 'Puff' and . . . stuff, 'kay?''

"Upstairs, Allison." Sam encouraged her departure with a firm hand at her back.

Holding Hunny by the tail, Allie dragged her feet all of the four tiny steps it took to reach the study door. She turned abruptly, inspiration shining in her expression. "Come upstairs with me, Glory, and Sam can read *The Best Nest* to you, too."

Sam scooped his daughter up under his arm. "I'll be right back," he said to Glory with a slightly embarrassed frown. "Don't, uh, go away."

"Not a chance." Her answer was bright and confident and Sam wondered what kind of chance he was taking by leaving her alone in his study for even a few minutes. "Don't worry about a thing," she continued with a smile. "I'll just clean up these papers and look around."

"I want Glory to sleep in my room," Allison said.

He looked down at the child draped over his arm and then back at Glory, who was already scanning the room with curious blue eyes. "I'll just be a minute," he said a little desperately. "Don't . . . touch anything."

"You can't read *The Best Nest* in just a minute," Allie complained as Sam started for the stairs. "It takes a bunch of minutes to do it right."

With a grim sort of urgency, he took the steps two at a time with Allison bouncing against his hip and

Hunny bobbling at his feet. As he reached the top of the stairs, a nerve-jangling clatter rattled out of the study, followed closely by an ominous "Oops."

Sam paused in dismay, but Allison began to squirm in his grasp. "You're squeezin' the breff out of me," she gasped.

He eased the pressure around her middle and hurried into her bedroom, dropping her onto the bed with little ceremony. "I'll be back to read *The Best Nest,*" he said quickly. "*Don't* get out of bed. If you so much as touch your toes to the floor before tomorrow morning, I promise you'll regret it."

"But what if I have to go to the bathroom?"

"I mean it, Allison." With that insubstantial threat, he hurried from the room, raced down the stairs, and came to a screeching halt inside the study. Glory was nowhere to be seen. The papers she had scattered on the floor were back on his desk, neatly stacked, looking for all the world as if they had never been disturbed. The glass he'd used earlier had been cleaned and put away and was now one of a dozen pieces of Waterford stemware that sparkled like ice on the bar behind his desk. He looked around for damage, something to match that jarring clatter he'd heard.

The French doors were open to the rose garden and he moved quickly to the threshold. "Glory?" he called, but he could see she wasn't in the garden. The night breeze twisted around him like a hungry kitten, teasing him with fleeting caresses and soft noises. She was gone, he thought with a twinge of disappointment. Gone. And he'd be very lucky if she hadn't taken anything of value with her.

"Damn!" He turned on his heel and walked— smack!—right into her. She tottered backward. In a futile grab to catch her before she went down, he lost his balance, too, and they fell together onto the hardwood floor. For a moment or two Sam was aware only of the body lying beneath him—the softness, the shape, the exquisite configuration of her female form. And then she began to stir, causing a whole new category of awareness. He pushed up so he could look down at her, and he discovered yet another danger in the sweet laughter that was gathering in her eyes.

"What happened?" she asked.

He was intrigued by the funny little dimple in her chin. "A close encounter of the third kind?"

"What?"

"Never mind. Just don't let me near any mashed potatoes." He rolled to the side and into a sitting position beside her, telling himself he had no business dwelling on her, uh, more charming aspects. "Are you all right?"

She pulled herself into a sitting position and adjusted the folds of her skirt. "Oh, sure. I may not be doing so well with the walking part, but I am definitely getting the hang of landing. If you like, I can give you a lesson."

"Thanks, but I'm afraid there won't be time. You're going to have to leave."

"I can't leave until my assignment is completed."

"It's all right. I'll explain everything to Mrs. Klepperson."

Her smile bloomed as coy as a winter rose. "I don't believe you understand who you're dealing with here, Sam."

He pushed to his feet and extended a hand down to her. "I'm sure you're right, but that doesn't change the fact that you have to leave."

Glory grabbed his hand with both of hers and rose unsteadily, clinging to him for balance. "I'm beginning to think you may be the toughest assignment I've ever had."

"You said I was your first assignment."

"At this rate, you'll be my last, and I'll find myself right back in the cherub corp."

"Cherub corp? What's that? Diaper duty?"

"More like designated driver." She sighed and looked into his eyes with a gently curious gaze. Then, unexpectedly, she lifted one hand and stroked his cheek. Her lips curved with surprise and obvious pleasure. "I didn't know touching a man would feel so nice."

He drew back, startled, and she grabbed his hand to keep from losing her balance again. "Whoa," she said. "That was almost another close encounter with those mashed potatoes. Do you think I could sit down?"

Before he could say no, she folded like a pair of deuces before a royal flush and sank, cross-legged, to the floor. She looked up with a smile. "You know, I think Leonard was right about this outfit. If I'd been wearing the leather, I'd have split my pants.''

Sam didn't know how to reply to that, but he knew he had to stop letting her distract him with her candid, come-hither allure. His first responsibility was to Allison and, no matter how innocent she looked, Glory was no angel. "Who the hell is Leonard?"

"His official title is Apprentice Angel Advisor in charge of in-body experience, but he's really just a troubleshooter for angels on assignment."

Sam nodded as if he understood. Either the nanny service was a haven for heavenly allegories or he was dealing with a real loony-toon. "Could I, maybe, talk to this . . . advisor?"

"Of course not," she said with a laugh. "He only talks to me and he only comes around if I get into trouble."

"Then I'm surprised I haven't already met him. By the way, what did you break?"

"Oh, don't worry, I fixed it."

"What?" he demanded, looking around the study for signs of destruction. "Fixed what?"

"Have you had your blood pressure checked lately? I think it may be a bit high."

And getting higher by the minute. "Damn it! I want you to get out of my house, and I want to know what the hell you demolished while I was upstairs with Allison!"

She shook her head sadly, setting the curls into fascinating motion about her face. "We're going to have to clean up your vocabulary, Sam. You do have an impressionable daughter, you know."

He scraped an impatient hand through his hair and wondered how he was supposed to deal with her. "I don't think you have any room to talk, Miss *Go-Getter.*"

She had the grace to blush. "First impressions are so important," she said with a sigh. "Maybe it would be best if you forgot that you'd seen me without clothes."

He didn't believe that was possible—and even if it were, he thought he just might prefer to keep that particular image on file in his memory bank. "If I promise to forget, will you promise to leave now, without creating a scene?"

She smiled and, for no reason he could fathom, he smiled back. "Allison is waiting for you," she said.

As if summoned by the statement, Allie's voice sailed down from her bedroom. "Sam? When are you gonna be through talking? Hunny is loosing his patience."

Glory lifted one delicate brow in mock alarm. "Uh-oh, you'd better get up there. Otherwise there'll be patience on the loose all over the place."

The strangest sensation wove into Sam's thoughts— a calm, sleepwalker kind of compulsion. He was aware of where he was and who he was and that Glory was with him. He knew he was on his way upstairs to read Allison a bedtime story before she fell asleep. Everything else, every other ambition, seemed surreal and vaguely unimportant, like dreams of a moonlit night.

"I'd better go upstairs now," he said, although he had every intention of staying downstairs until this woman was safely out of his house.

"It's never good to keep a dragon waiting."

A wonderful lethargy stole over his body, pilfering bits and pieces of his determination like a petty thief. "What are you going to do?"

"Oh, I'll be around." With a sweep of her hand, she indicated her lotus position on the floor. "Since I'm down here, I may as well do a little meditating on the art of putting one foot in front of the other. Don't give me another thought, Sam. At least, not until tomorrow."

He nodded an acceptance he didn't exactly feel, but couldn't quite deny. And then he walked away from her as if she weren't even there.

Chapter Three

Pristine sunbeams streamed through the back door window, bisecting the kitchen tiles into a cheerful mosaic. Sam did a couple of lazy stretches in the doorway, then padded barefoot across the sun-checked linoleum to the sink. Bracing his hands against the countertop, he limbered up with another stretch, then yawned long and pleasurably. He couldn't recall the last time he'd slept so soundly and awakened so rested—or so late. The clock radio beside the sink ticked off a count of the seconds—seven-oh-eight and fifteen seconds . . . sixteen . . . seventeen. . . . In self-defense, Sam reached out and flipped on the radio.

The rowdy prattle of Jenny's favorite airwaves jockey was an abrupt reminder of how vibrant and alive this kitchen had been at one time, how full of the early news and weather and daily nonsense. Not much music, but then Jenny had always said she wanted to know what she'd missed during the night, not hear the umpteenth playing of a record she hadn't even liked the first time she'd heard it.

Sam turned the dial—looking for the first station, the first sound, that didn't remind him of the past—and found a soothing voice. "Retained with these exercises. However, dreams can be, and often are, recalled hours later even without the mental cues we discussed on today's show."

"All right, listeners, line up those mental cues now and start the leg lifts...and a one and a two...oh-kay! Keep your dial on 92.3 because tomorrow, on your KBOZ Dream Team Station, Dr. Grace Tracy will give us a few rules of thumb on how to interpret our drea—"

Sam gave the dial another twirl and came up with a nerve-jarring combination of bass and electric guitar. That would certainly browbeat the silence into a manageable distraction, he thought, and switched off the radio. At worst, the silence would only last until Allie got up, anyway. Which brought back the memory of Mrs. Maggard's abrupt departure and the annoying recollection that, barring a miracle, he would be taking his five-year-old, and her whole bag of distractions, to the office with him. Maybe he should call another agency. Mrs. Klepperson's guardian angels weren't the only nannies in Tulsa.

Oh, I never had any clothes to begin with. The memory of words and laughter wove like ribbons all around his sudden mental picture of a woman—a very beautiful, very nude, woman. And just that quickly, last night's dream came back to him in all its vivid, tantalizing images. Sam lifted a hand to massage the back of his neck. He'd never had a dream like that before. A dream so real he felt the oddest compulsion to....

He turned to look at the back door. It was absurd to check the patio, comical even to entertain the idea that there had been someone out there last night. He'd probably heard the neighbors' basset hound rattling the garbage cans and that had somehow fed into his dream and become a naked nanny. *Naked nanny*. Two mutually exclusive words, if he'd ever heard any. Half ashamed of himself for being so gullible, he walked over and looked through the window at the backyard.

Not a scrap of litter marred the dew-drenched grass. Not so much as a tuna can cluttered the patio. The four trash containers stood in their customary places, with lids attached, undefiled by so much as Ethel's footprint. Sam released a breath of self-conscious laughter, which turned cold on his lips when the doorbell chimed a familiar chorus.

I love that song. Her face, her smile, both were as vivid in his mind as the words. Sam shook his head and moved purposely across the kitchen and into the hall. The past week had been stressful for him, what with moving Allie home and trying to reinstate his presence in her life while searching for the perfect nanny—who, once found, had subsequently left him high and dry.

"Puff" is a beautiful song.... Her name was Glory and she had the voice of an angel.

Like a drowning man, Sam reached for the door-knob and jerked open the door.

"Good lookin' undershirt, Sam, but here in the Midwest, we wear shirts and ties to work. Shoes and socks, too." Damon Field, business partner and friend, sailed past Sam and headed for the kitchen. "You're running behind schedule, my man. And here I got out of bed twenty minutes early so I could stop on the way over and pick up your breakfast." He held up two white bakery sacks and rattled them invitingly. "Jelly doughnuts and apple fritters for us and a couple dozen doughnut holes for the Princess of Pout."

Sam closed the door and followed Damon down the hall and into the kitchen. "The way you tease her, it's no wonder Allison pouts when you're around."

"She loves to be teased." Damon pursed his lips as he set the bakery sacks on the table. "Shouldn't you crank it into third gear? The meeting with Morrison is at eight and you know what a Missouri mule he is about starting on time."

"I'm aware of the time and the importance of the meeting, but I have something of a . . . small problem this morning."

Damon cuffed Sam on the shoulder. "You know how I hate bein' the one to say 'I told you so,' but I did warn you that you couldn't handle a kid and a house and a fifty-two-hour work week. You should have left Allie with her grandmother and just brought her here on weekends and holidays. That arrangement worked out pretty good this last year, didn't it? I mean, it gave you both time to recover after the funeral. And it wasn't like you wanted to spend most of the year in Europe. You didn't have a choice."

"I shouldn't have done it." Sam battled the guilt that never quite left him alone. Leaving Allie had been selfish and wrong, the worst decision of several he'd made right after Jenny's death. Grief and work had been convenient, unarguable excuses, but neither had been the real reason. He'd been scared. Flat-out, deep-in-the-gut scared. Scared of a life without the woman he'd loved since he was thirteen. Scared of a home that no longer had a heart. Scared of a role he didn't know how to fill. So he'd run. As fast and as far as he could. "I shouldn't have left her."

"You did the right thing, Sam. Janice and Jim loved having her with them. Besides, a construction site in Italy—or anywhere else for that matter—is no place for a kid." He rubbed his hands together and surveyed the kitchen. "Now, if you'll stop beating yourself up long enough to point me in the right direction, I'll try to squeeze a decent cup of java out of that aluminum monster Jenny lovingly referred to as a coffeemaker."

"The Tank and Tummy Quick Mart has coffee for fifty-nine cents a cup," Sam suggested. "And it's right on the way to the office."

"Come on, Sammy, you're not going to let a machine get the best of you." He pulled open a cabinet door and nodded in satisfaction. "Remember when we took apart your dad's video camera? We got that back together, didn't we?''

''As I recall, we very nearly died a slow and painful death over that.''

With a clank and clatter loud enough to wake the neighbors, Damon pulled the always-ready, perfect-to-the-last-drop, no-fuss brewmeister out of the cabinet and wrestled it to the counter. ''But we didn't die, did we?'' That was always the bottom line for Damon. The worst thing that didn't happen.

Sam eyed the coffeemaker and Damon's efforts to master it. At the moment, a good cup of coffee sounded like a bit of heaven, but he'd had five mornings' worth of experience with the brewmeister, and he knew there wasn't a chance in hell of getting the thing to work. Jenny could have—if she'd been here to do it. ''It's a lost cause, Damon. There's milk in the refrigerator. Drink that. Maybe the calcium will dilute some of the grease you're getting ready to dump into your stomach.''

''I'm having coffee,'' Damon said with the single-minded, short-term determination for which he was famous. ''You go get your shirt on and I'll—'' He straightened as his gaze fell on the doorway. ''Well, if it isn't the little princess. Good morning, Your Highness.''

Allison sniffed a regal disdain for his teasing. ''Hunny and I are ready for breakfast,'' she said to Sam.

"I brought doughnut holes." Damon pointed to one of the sacks. "Bet you can't eat just one."

Sam pulled out a chair at the table and Allie climbed onto it. "Hunny wants applesauce," she said. "And I want a hamburger."

Sam scooted the chair closer to the table. "Cherry or strawberry popper pastry?"

Allie sighed and laid her head on the table. "I don't want a popper pastee," she mumbled into her hand. "I want a hamburger and French fries and lots of pickles."

"Cherry, it is." Sam moved to the cabinet and took out the toaster, the one appliance in the kitchen he could trust. "You want one, Damon?"

"Make mine strawberry." Damon plugged in the brewmeister, flipped on the switch, and dusted his hands in a gesture of accomplishment before he pulled out the chair opposite Allison's, turned it around and straddled it, facing her. "So, Princess, you ready to trade that worthless piece of dragon skin for my stuffed bobcat?"

Allie lifted her head. "We have a garden angel. And if I tell her to, she'll make you disappear."

"Ooooo." Damon waggled his eyebrows in mock alarm. "A garden angel. Does she have a green thumb and carrot-colored hair?"

Sam pushed up the lever on the toaster, unconcerned if breakfast wasn't exactly piping hot as long as he got something stuffed in between him and the war that was about to erupt in his kitchen. "Two popper pastries coming right up."

"Come on, Allie," Damon teased. "I'll give you a bite of my jelly doughnut if you tell me about the garden angel. Does she have a cauliflower ear and an onion for a nose?"

Sam set a plate in front of Allison and slid another across the table to his daughter's tormenter. "Leave her alone, Damon. She's talking about the nanny. Mrs. Maggard was from the Guardian Angel agency."

Damon had a talent for picking out definitive words and it didn't fail him now. "What do you mean *was*?"

"Mrs. Maggard left to pursue...happiness or something."

"Me and Hunny aleeated her."

Sam looked at his daughter in quiet desperation. Where did she come up with these ideas? "I think you misunderstood, Allison. Mrs. Maggard didn't leave because of anything you did."

The child propped the dragon's floppy head on the table before she took a big bite out of the popper pastry. "It's okay, Sam," she said around the mouthful of food. "Me and Hunny like Glory better, anyways."

I'm Glory. I'm your guardian angel. No. Wait. That was his dream. How could Allison—?

"Hell-o." Damon's softly spoken warning sent a ripple of alarm coursing through Sam. He turned toward the door as Damon pushed to his feet, scraping the chair legs on the linoleum. "Sam, old man," Damon whispered under his breath, "you have been holding out on me. *Who* is this?"

This was the woman. The one from his dream. She stood in the doorway, a sundress of vivid blue draped like spring over her lovely body. With one hand braced against the doorjamb and the other holding a beribboned hat, she looked like an advertisement for champagne...or anything intoxicating. She smiled and he would have sworn the sunbeams brightened. "Isn't this beautiful morning a miracle?" she said.

"A miracle," Damon echoed. "You must be the garden angel."

"I'm Glory."

Sam took a step toward her, unsure of what, exactly, he knew about her and what, exactly, he'd dreamed. He remembered her, he was sure of that. Remembered the dream, he was pretty sure of that, too. But if she were a dream, how could she be standing in his kitchen? And if she weren't a dream....
"Where did you come from?" he asked hoarsely.

"Straight out of my dreams." Damon moved like a predator and was at the doorway in the blink of an eye. "I'm Damon Field. No doubt Sam has told you about me, even though he somehow neglected to tell me about you."

"Damon," she said, and the sound glistened like a dewdrop. "I know about you."

"Whatever he's told you is exaggerated and mostly not true."

"Some of it's true. That's a very nice suit."

Damon was flattered to the soles of his top-dollar, custom-made shoes—and didn't try to hide it. "You have a discerning eye."

"Do you think so? I'm really trying to figure out this style thing."

Damon's appreciative gaze swept over her. "Style is something you're born with. And believe me, angel, you were born well endowed."

"Actually, I was created." She stopped leaning against the doorjamb and took a careful step into the room, a smile in her eyes. "Good morning, Sam. Is it time for breakfast?"

Sam couldn't take his eyes off her, couldn't sort his thoughts into any kind of order. He didn't know what she was doing in his house or why she seemed so comfortable in it. He did know there were questions he ought to be asking, answers he should be demanding, but when he opened his mouth, not a single syllable surfaced.

"Want a popper pastee, Glory?" Allie mumbled through a mouthful. "You could have some of Hunny's applesauce, 'cept nobody's gived him any."

"Given," Sam corrected automatically.

"Well, he must be starving." Glory settled the hat on her head and tied the wide ribbon in a pretty bow under her chin. "I'll get it for him." She took two steps toward the refrigerator before her bare feet slid right out from under her and, with a soft, surprised little gasp, she landed—plop!—right in Sam's arms.

He caught her on the strength of reflex alone and bent with her sudden weight, winding up with his lips only inches from the neckline of the blue dress, a mere breath away from an exquisite, gently curving, expanse of creamy skin. Slowly he lifted his head and found his gaze captured by the sight of shiny blue ribbons framing the tempting slope of her throat. He followed the edge of the ribbon to the dainty outline of her ear, then across the delicate tint of color in her cheek to eyes of a mysterious blue, half hidden behind long, sooty lashes, and then down to a pair of enticing, slightly parted lips. For a single, breathless moment, his thoughts were willing hostages of a longing he wouldn't allow himself to recognize. From this perspective, he had no idea what he'd wanted to ask her. Hell, from this perspective, he had no idea how to talk.

"I'm still having a little trouble with these feet," she said. "Thanks for catching me."

"I seem to have a knack for it." Acutely conscious of curious eyes watching his every movement, he set Glory on her feet and steadied her with his hands at her waist. She felt infinitely feminine within the circle of his fingers, and he recalled that it had been a long time since he'd touched a woman like this and imagined the silken feel of her skin against his. He dropped his hands to his sides. "I'd better get the applesauce."

"What do you think of my outfit?" she asked as if one subject were relevant to the other. "I picked it out of a coloring book."

"Well, you did a great job of staying in the lines." Sam opened the refrigerator and forced himself to stop staring at her. He'd figure this out. Any minute now, everything would make sense.

"But do you like it?" When she'd fallen, the hat had slipped and now hovered below the crown of her head, held in place by the ribbons tied at her throat, framing her buttercup curls in a halo of straw. "I didn't know if I should wear the hat."

"It's perfectly charming." Damon stepped closer. "You're a delight from head to toe."

Bare toes, Sam thought. Bare from head to toe. Wait a minute. He glanced at the back door and tried to grab on to details of the dreamlike encounter that scooted through his memory like the tail of a comet. Last night, on the patio, she hadn't been wearing any clothes. He slammed the refrigerator door. "There are a couple of things I need to discuss with you, Glory," he said tightly. "Could I see you in my study?"

"You don't have time for a tête-à-tête, Sam," Damon protested. "Go put your shirt on. Finish getting ready." In a lazy display of chivalry, he pulled out a chair for Glory. "Don't worry about a thing. Allie and I will fill your garden angel in on the house rules, won't we, Princess?"

Allie wiggled around in her chair and peered at Sam through the slats. "*Pleezzzeee* get the applesauce, 'fore Hunny starts gettin' mad."

Glory sat down and then looked directly into Sam's eyes. "There is nothing to worry about," she said softly. "I'm here to help you and I'm not going to break any rules."

Sam frowned. A second ago words had been burning a hole in his tongue. Now, suddenly, all he could taste was the smile forming on his lips. "Have some breakfast," he said, which was not at all what he'd intended to say. "We'll talk later."

"I think you're finally starting to wake up and smell the coffee, Sammy. Now, if you'd just shake a leg, maybe we can get to the office before Morrison does." Damon straddled his chair again and admired Glory across the table.

With a sigh twice her size, Allison slid from her chair and walked to the refrigerator. "Applesauce," she said with exaggerated patience. "When is Hunny going to get his *damn* applesauce?"

Sam was shocked out of his reverie. "Allison Jill Oliver! Where did you hear that word?"

Her chin quivered. "You say it every morning, Sam. Every time *that* happens." She pointed toward the counter where the always-ready, perfect-to-the-last-drop, no-fuss brewmeister hissed ominously.

"Damn—Damon!" Sam caught the word and made a quick substitution as he bolted for the electrical outlet. "I told you this thing wouldn't work. I've got to unplug it before—"

With an angry gurgle, the brewmeister turned into a coffee volcano, spewing coffee and coffee grounds across the counter, spraying the cabinets and wall with a brown drizzle, spattering the floor—and Sam's beige slacks—with a fine mist of coffee stains. Sam looked at the electric plug he now held in his hand and told himself he wouldn't say the word. Not in front of Allison. Not again. No matter how frustrated he felt. No matter how much he wanted to say...

"Damn," Damon supplied in a voice of wonder. "It really doesn't work, does it?"

Sam rubbed the ache that was forming at the back of his neck. "It's never exploded like this before, but I haven't gotten a decent cup of coffee out of it, either."

"Maybe you should try drinking fruit juice instead."

He turned slowly, brewmeister cord in hand, all the morning's frustrations banding together, to meet Glory's perky suggestion. "Coffeemakers are supposed to brew water and coffee beans and produce coffee. I like coffee. I don't like fruit juice."

She shrugged. "That's a shame because juice has a bunch of vitamins, and I was really looking forward to having a healthy body while I'm here."

Damon was on his feet in an instant. "A body as fine as yours deserves to be healthy. Sam? Don't you have an electric juicer?"

"Don't even think about it." Sam tossed the electrical cord onto the counter next to the brewmeister. "I'm going upstairs to change. Damon, if you want to make that meeting with Morrison, you'll have this mess cleaned up by the time I get back."

He started for the door, but Allie planted herself in his path. "What about Hunny's breakfast?"

Sam made an abrupt detour to the refrigerator, took out a quart jar, set it on the table, and stuck a spoon into the applesauce. "Get your dragon fed, Allie. Then run upstairs and get dressed as fast as you can. You're coming to work with me this morning."

Half on, half off the chair, she looked up and blinked in pleased surprise. "I am?"

"She is?" Damon echoed in dismay.

"She is." Sam left the room, proud that he hadn't even glanced at Glory in passing, uneasily aware that if he had he might have lost control of his tongue again and done something completely unpredictable and incredibly stupid—like inviting her to go with them.

He didn't understand what had happened to him in the past few hours. Somewhere between dusk and dawn, he'd gotten tangled up in a dream, lost touch with reality, and fallen under some kind of witch's spell. He wasn't sure what he'd seen, what he'd dreamed, or that he wasn't hallucinating. He knew he had no explanation for Glory's presence in his house this morning. And yet, here she was, charming his daughter and his friend, cheering his dreary kitchen with her smile, creating a conflict between his heart and his head.

She had to be one of the Guardian Angel nannies, though he couldn't imagine why Mrs. Klepperson hadn't phoned to inform him she'd changed her mind and was sending someone after all. Not that it mattered. Glory was totally unsuitable. He didn't need to stop and consider all the things he didn't know about her to realize that he shouldn't allow her to stay another minute.

Sam reached his bedroom and the obvious conclusion at the same time. He'd ask her to leave in such a manner that there could be no misunderstanding. He'd be firm, but adamant. He'd be sympathetic to her arguments, but steadfast in his decision. No matter how sweetly she smiled at him.

"YOU'LL COME WITH US, of course." The words dropped into the quiet of his study like an atom bomb. Sam knew it was his voice, could feel the warmth of the words on his lips, even though he had had no earthly intention of issuing such an invitation. Quite the opposite, in fact. He shook his head. "I can't believe I just said that."

Glory smiled at him. "Oh, you'll get used to it. Technically, I'm not supposed to put words in your mouth, but I'm allowed a certain amount of leeway at first." She shifted her position in the chair and the skirt of the blue sundress parted at the button-front panel, revealing one shapely leg crossed over the other.

Sam was uncomfortably aware that he should leave his perch on the corner of the desk before the calf of his leg came into contact with her very attractive ankle. He didn't make a move, however, and he wasn't sure if that were his fault or hers. "Look," he began, "I don't know how you do that little 'Bewitched' routine, but it isn't going to work on me anymore. I do intend to hire another nanny, but it won't be you because, quite frankly, you're not suited for the job."

"I can change." She began to swing her hat back and forth, the ribbons curling around her fingers in bright, blue stripes. "I probably should put on something more appropriate since we're going to your office."

"No, no, no." Sam leaned toward her. "I wasn't talking about your clothes."

"I was afraid of that." She sighed. "The hat's too much, isn't it? I should have chosen something more conservative."

Sam hadn't wanted to mention their initial encounter on the patio, but subtlety didn't seem to be helping him make his point. "You could put on a nun's habit and I still wouldn't hire you. The truth is..." He fumbled just this side of being blunt. "The truth is, first impressions are hard to ignore, and last night you made one hell of a first impression."

The hat stopped swinging. "Are you still thinking about that?"

"Well... I can't just overlook the fact that you showed up at my back door without any clothes on."

"I thought you weren't talking about my clothes."

"I'm talking about the fact that last night you weren't wearing any."

"But I told you, I forgot them."

"People don't *forget* to wear clothes."

"Well, angels do," she said sharply. "I don't understand how you can still remember that part when I specifically asked you not to."

"Glory, I saw you *naked*. That's not something a prospective employer is apt to forget."

Frown lines settled on her brow. "Are you saying there's something wrong with my body?"

"No!" *Hell, no.* "I'm saying I shouldn't have seen it."

She rolled her eyes toward the ceiling. "Either you're trying to confuse me, or I didn't pay enough attention during biology lessons. I thought the human body was considered an object of beauty."

"It is. I mean, it is beautiful in...well, in art and...uh, certain other...situations."

"Sex, you mean."

Sam ran a finger under his shirt collar. "That would be one of the situations, yes. However, we're not talking about those times when clothing is optional. We're talking about totally inappropriate behavior for a nanny."

"Then I guess I won't be a nanny."

Finally. Sam gave a silent sigh of relief, then he stood and offered his hand, thinking that a handshake would wrap up this odd interlude once and for all.

She looked at his hand and then looped the ribbons of her hat over his outstretched palm. "I won't be needing a hat where I'm going."

The ribbons were still warm from her touch, and he closed his fingers around them as if he were cradling her hand. "I know it's none of my business, but where are you going?"

She rose slowly and looked him square in the eyes. "I'm going with you, Sam. You invited me. Remember?"

"Hey, Sam," Damon called from the back of the house. "Let's go. We're barely going to beat Morrison to the office as it is."

"I can't find my socks," Allie yelled down the stairs.

Sam didn't let his gaze waver from Glory's. "It won't work this time. You're not putting any more words in my mouth, you're not going to my office, and you're not staying in my house. I am not about to let—"

With a wave of her hand, Glory called for time out and everything stopped, including the monotonous click, click, click of the clock on Sam's desk. She sank down into the chair and drummed her fingers against the curved wooden arm as she contemplated her options.

Sam towered over her, frozen in mid-moment, completely unaware that she had interrupted his lecture. Even in unanimated stillness, he was incredibly beautiful. Handsome, she corrected. Men were handsome. Strong and muscular. Women were beautiful. And the naked human body was beautiful...but only in art and sex and when clothing was optional. Glory sighed. Oh, she was never going to get this all figured out.

"I need some help here, Leonard."

Instantly, it was done. The clock resumed its countdown, and Sam finished his sentence. "You and Allison stay here alone until I've had a chance to explain your duties and responsibilities. Now, if you'll go upstairs and help Allie find her socks, I'll get my briefcase and we'll be on our way."

"Very well, Mr. Oliver." Glory walked to the doorway, taking extra care with each step so as not to trip and accidentally jog his memory. Placing her hand on the door frame for balance, she turned to face him again. "I do have one question."

His lips curved up at the corners even though the furrows across his brow indicated a frown. "Yes?"

"Is this outfit appropriate to wear to your office?"

His eyes flickered from the high collar of her prim white blouse, to the uncompromising fit of her conservative gray skirt, to the practical thick-soled brogans covering her feet, and back to the granny glasses perched halfway down her nose, and the neat, very nannylike bun on top of her head. He nodded with no hint of enthusiasm. "Very stylish."

Glory managed a dutiful smile as she put one clod-hoppered foot in front of the other and started—carefully—up the stairs. "Leonard," she muttered under her breath, "for an angel, you have a wicked sense of humor."

Chapter Four

The blare of a car horn burst into the study like a wild man, demanding action. Sam straightened the knot of his tie, adjusted the sleeves of his suit jacket, and looked around the familiar study. He could not seem to shake the feeling that he was forgetting something. Something important. Another quick scan of his desk didn't bring anything to mind, and with a pensive frown, he picked up his briefcase and headed for the front door.

"Sam! Look, Sam." Allie's excited voice called to him from the top of the stairs, and he turned as she rounded the landing and galloped down the remaining steps. "Glory put a bow in my hair. A red bow."

He ignored the press of time to smile at his daughter. "Are you sure that isn't a butterfly on your head?"

She pressed her hand to her hip. "It's a bow. Can't you see?"

"Hmm, let me take a closer look." He stooped down, cupped her chin in his hand, and turned her head from side to side so he could give the hair bow his careful consideration. Her smile was sweet with self-satisfaction, and Sam absorbed her pleasure as if it were something he'd earned. "You're right. It is a red bow and you look positively stunning in it."

"Ohhhh..." She patted the bow with careful delight. "What's stunning?"

"It means beautiful."

"Then Glory is stunning, too." Allison directed her smile over her shoulder and Sam followed her lead.

He felt a warm flush of attraction as his gaze fell on the very beautiful woman who stood on the second stair, her hand gracing the dark wood of the banister like inlaid ivory. It was hard to believe this was the same woman he'd interviewed in his study not ten minutes ago. Gone were the clunky shoes, replaced by a neat pair of penny loafers. The shapeless skirt had given way to a trim pair of tan slacks. Her blouse was open at the throat and its stark whiteness had been softened by the addition of a patchwork vest. Her hair was loose, framing her piquant face in a flurry of haphazard curls. She was watching him with a kind of uncertain curiosity. "Allie and I are ready to go," she said. "We hurried so you wouldn't be late for your meeting."

"I thought you wore glasses" was the only thing he could think of to say.

Her smile was as quick as her shrug. "I changed."

The car horn once again sounded impatiently and Sam rose to open the front door. "All right, ladies.

Let's go before Damon becomes a real public nuisance."

Swinging her tote bag in a wide arc, Allie bounced past Sam and down the front steps like a little red ball of energy. "We're going to the office," she sang. "We're going to the office."

Glory approached the doorway at a measured pace and paused outside on the porch to wait for Sam while he set the alarm and locked the door. "She's almost as excited as I am. I've never been to an office before, you know."

Sam raised an eyebrow, but decided not to ask. The less personal conversation he had with her, the better their employer/employee relationship would be. And no matter how attractive she was, he was her employer. He had hired her to be Allison's nanny based on her qualifications...even though at the moment his memory was a little fuzzy as to just what those qualifications were. "You and Allison have something in common, then," he said. "She's never been before, either."

"She's never been to your office?"

"No." That fact hadn't seemed odd to him until just now.

"Why not? Is it...dangerous?"

"Not unless you try to shred government documents." He smiled, but she didn't. "I'm only kidding. Allie's never been to my office because there wasn't...well, she didn't..." Allie hadn't been to the office with him because she was too young. She was still too young, come to think of it. "I do expect you to keep her entertained and out of the way this morning. This meeting is extremely important."

"I understand perfectly. Don't worry about a thing. You won't even know we're in the same building."

Sam smiled a dubious encouragement and hoped she was at least half as efficient at her job as she was at changing her appearance. As they started down the steps, he reached out to take her arm, as naturally as he might have reached out to Jenny. He didn't understand what impulse had prompted the action or why he wanted to touch her. And yet his hand remained cupped at her elbow, he remained at her side, solicitous, supportive, entirely too sensitive to the rhythmic movement of her body beside him and the vibrant energy that surrounded her. Not a great way to begin this strictly business relationship, he thought, and then still had to practically tear his fingers from her arm.

Damon gave the car horn a couple of short honks as he waved at them from the driver's side. "Could you throw it into overdrive?" he called. "Allie's going to outgrow her safety seat before you two get in the car."

"Car?" Excitement sparkled in Glory's voice. "Is that a sports car?"

Sam felt a twinge of irritation at her enthusiasm. "I suppose that depends on whether you ask Damon or me. He calls it a midsize coupe, but I say it has all the markings of a midlife crisis."

"I am not old enough to have a midlife crisis," Damon said with a smug nod. "You're just jealous because you drive a station wagon that's in the shop more often than not lately. I've been trying to talk him into buying a new car, Glory, but he's sentimental about that old wagon.''

"Not sentimental. Practical. It makes more sense to drive a car I can trust.''

"Would that *trusted* car be the same tired old wagon you left at Danny's Auto Repair last week?''

"All cars need routine maintenance, and you know as well as I do that when I drive it out of the shop, it'll be good for at least another fifty thousand miles.''

"Oh, at least.'' Damon wiped a minute smudge off the spit-polished hood of his shiny new car. "But think of the excitement, the thrill you could be experiencing if you were behind the wheel of a premium vehicle like this baby.''

"Just thinking of it gives me heartburn.'' Sam opened the passenger door and leaned down to release the seat lock so Glory could climb into the rear seat with Allison. He liked his reliable and roomy wagon much better than this turbo-charged sardine can. Jenny had loved the station wagon, and there was no doubt in Sam's mind that she would have hated this latest and most expensive of Damon's toys.

"It's so... tempting.'' Glory admired the machine with a careful stroke of her fingers. "Like a shiny red apple.''

Damon laughed. "Well, this apple is turbo-charged, fuel-injected, with five on the floor, T-tops and every electronic gadget known to General Motors.''

"I bet you have so much fun with it."

"That, darlin', is a magnificent understatement." Damon tossed the keys in the air and caught them with a swipe of his hand. "Would you like to drive?"

Sam bumped his head on the car roof.

"Would I!" Glory said with enthusiasm.

"Got your license to fly?" Damon asked with a laugh.

"I never leave Heaven without it."

"Great. You don't mind sitting in back with Allison, do you, Sam?" Damon was already heading around the front of the car, passing Glory, who was on her way to the driver's side.

Sam rubbed the back of his head and gave his buddy a skeptical frown. "I thought we were in a hurry," he said tersely.

"Who says she can't get us there as fast as I can?" Damon sent Glory a wink and a thumbs-up across the hood of the car. "Maybe faster."

Sam watched Glory get in the car. "Come on, Damon. Do you really think this is a good idea? You barely know her and you're letting her drive your car."

"You barely know her and you're letting her take care of your kid."

An irrefutable point that brought a flash of memory, a trace of a conversation Sam couldn't quite recall—a hazy image he wanted to remember, but couldn't. "The agency wouldn't have sent her if she didn't meet their high standards of qualification and character."

Damon cuffed Sam on the shoulder. "And if she weren't a gorgeous blonde, you can be certain I wouldn't let her drive my car, either. I have my standards, too, you know." He turned back to the car. "All set, angels?"

"Let's go." Allie rocked against the harness of her safety seat. "Let's go."

"Waiting on you." Glory ran her hands over the steering wheel as if it were made of gold.

Damon waggled his eyebrows. "When's the last time a gorgeous blonde asked to drive your station wagon, Mr. Practical?"

Feeling disgruntled and out of sorts, Sam crawled into the rear seat without comment.

"Comfy?" Damon chuckled as he righted the back of the seat—clipping Sam in the knees—and then settled into the passenger side next to Glory. "Got plenty of room back there?"

Sam tried to find a comfortable compromise between the space he needed for his long legs and the meager allotment of inches between the edge of his seat and the back side of the seat in which Damon was sitting. Allison's giggle caught him unaware, and he glanced over to see her hiding her laughter behind her hand. "All right," he said, finding a single ray of good humor glinting like sunshine through the clouds of his frustration. "Just what are you laughing at, Allie?"

Her hand dropped from her mouth and her little-girl giggles filled him, heart and soul, with a nearly forgotten happiness.

"You're sitting on Hunny's tail." She pointed to the dragon on the seat between them. "And you didn't even know it."

"Well, he should have said something." Sam pulled the tail end of the dragon out from behind him and then settled back in the cramped seat. "No wonder I didn't have enough room."

"Fasten seat belts." Glory adjusted the rearview mirror and smiled at the two occupants in the back. "Everybody buckled in back there?"

Allie nodded a vigorous confirmation. "Ready for blastoff."

Damon checked his watch. "We're at fifteen minutes and counting. Do you think you can make it?"

"I've been around the world and back in less time," Glory assured him with a cocky toss of her head. "Now, how do I get this chariot to go?"

Sam couldn't help feeling a little smug as a flicker of concern crossed Damon's face. "Just push in the clutch and turn the key," Damon said. "You, uh, have driven a five-speed before, haven't you, Glory?"

The engine purred to life at her touch and she uttered a silky laugh of satisfaction. "Trust me, Damon. You have never been in better hands."

"WATCH OUT for that red light."

"What's it going to do?"

"When the light is red, you're...supposed...to... *Stop!*" Damon plowed his foot into the floorboard.

Sam squeezed his eyes shut against the imminent crash.

"There is no need to panic," Glory said as the car glided through the intersection on a green light. "I have everything under control."

"Holy moley," Damon said. "I think you must be a natural."

"A natural disaster," Sam muttered under his sigh of relief. He debated whether to pray for divine intervention or to give his partner a well-deserved pop in the jaw. He leaned forward and jabbed Damon in the arm. "You need a new set of standards."

Glory glanced back and caught Sam's eye. "I'm not making you nervous, am I?"

In answer, Sam checked Allison's safety straps and then cinched his own seat belt another notch. "Nervous? Oh, no. I'm just speechless at the way you're able to court catastrophe."

"Why, thanks, Sam." She flashed him a smile and then, with a bit of guidance from Damon, she shifted into fifth gear. "I think I'm handling this little apple pretty well, myself."

"Evel Knievel couldn't do any better." Damon patted her hand with his. "Today, the Broken Arrow Expressway. Tomorrow, the Indy 500."

Sam suppressed a groan and itemized the reasons he had to be nervous. He was scrunched in the back seat of a little red car that had miraculously escaped several near collisions in the past five minutes. He was late for an important meeting. He was taking his daughter *and* her new nanny to his office with him. Or rather the new nanny was taking him—and this journey could well be his last.

Oh, he had good cause to feel nervous, but oddly, the only thing that concerned him at the moment was the sight of Damon's hand resting on top of Glory's on the gearshift. He didn't like that. Didn't like it by half. And nervousness had nothing to do with it.

"I like the way you drive, Glory," Allie said. "And so does Hunny."

"And so do I." Damon, who hadn't had the common sense to turn pale during this journey, patted and squeezed her hand. "Don't mind Sam. He wasn't built for speed and adventure."

Definitely a pop in the jaw, Sam thought. At the first opportunity.

"GOOD MORNING! Isn't this a beautiful day?" Glory leaned through the open window to greet the dour-faced policeman as he approached the car.

In the back seat, Sam rubbed the tension that was throbbing behind his eyes and wondered what else could go wrong before eight o'clock.

"Anything wrong, Officer?" Damon asked in a slightly strangled voice. "We were just, uh, on our way to the office."

"Insurance verification?" The officer gave the words an authoritarian snap as his gaze took in the seat-belted passengers and the child safety seat in which Allison was sitting. Damon rummaged through the glove box and came up with the requested document.

"That is a smart-looking uniform," Glory said appreciatively as she passed the paper through the window. "I really like the boots. And the sunglasses . . . could I try those on?"

The officer's expression darkened considerably. "I need to see your driver's license, please."

She laughed as if his no-nonsense words indicated he actually had a sense of humor. "Don't be silly. I'm just learning to drive. I don't have a license."

Damon let out a low groan, and even though Sam knew it was somewhat childish, he began to plan just how he would say "I told you so."

"Student driver." The policeman began making notes on his ticket pad. "Driving at the speed of light without a license."

"Apprentice."

The officer stopped writing to look at her. "What?"

She reached up and tapped her finger on the notation he'd made. "You should have written apprentice angel, not student driver."

"Apprentice angel," the officer repeated with a cynical nod of his helmeted head. "And I suppose you simply mistook this shiny red sports car for a fiery chariot."

Glory turned to flash her smile on Damon. "Sam was right," she said. "It *is* a sports car."

Sam leaned forward to try to make eye contact with the policeman. "She works for a local personnel service," he explained. "The Guardian Angel Nanny Service."

The policeman bent down and frowned through the open window at Sam. "Who are you?" he asked.

"That's Sam." Allie held up her dragon. "This is Hunny. He bites."

"Allison." Sam growled at her from the side of his mouth.

"Well, he does."

"How old are you, young lady?" the officer asked Allie.

"Five and old enough to un'erstand."

"Understand what?"

"Un'erstand that there's *work* to be done and that you're a copper and you're gonna put us all in jail."

Copper? Sam massaged his temple. Where did she hear these words?

"No one is going to jail, Allison." Glory reached back and squeezed Allie's foot reassuringly before she turned her bright, fearless smile on the policeman. "Isn't that right, Officer Hickman?"

"No one is going to jail, Allison." Officer Hickman dutifully repeated the words as he tore the ticket from his pad and shredded it into pieces. "I'm just out here this morning reminding people to enjoy the beautiful day." He chuckled as he poured the ticket scraps into Glory's cupped hands. "Now, take your time and admire the wildflowers planted along the roadside." He stepped away from the car and touched the edge of his helmet as if he were tipping a hat. "You all enjoy this lovely morning or I'll have to write you a real ticket, you hear?''

Glory dusted her hands and the scraps of paper floated away, drifting and darting like butterflies over the wildflower plot beside the expressway. Wait a minute. Sam strained for a closer look. Those *were* butterflies.

"Thank you, Officer Hickman," Glory said. "You're a credit to that fine uniform."

He took off the sunglasses, revealing a pair of friendly—if slightly dazed—gray eyes. "Here—" he offered the sunglasses to Glory "—you can have these. I can always get another pair."

"Oh, that's so nice of you, but really, I don't need dark glasses. I'm accustomed to bright light. Thank you, anyway, and you have a wonderful day." Glory started the car and watched in the side mirror as Officer Hickman returned to his motorcycle. "Wasn't that a pleasant interruption?" she asked. "I guess we'd better make tracks for the office, though, if we still want to get there before eight, huh?"

She turned her head to look first at Damon and then at Sam, who were both studying her with expressions that mixed astonishment, awe, and suspicion. "What?" she said. "Don't tell me you two thought he was actually going to give me a ticket?"

"I thought we all were going *down—town*." Damon stressed both syllables of the word and then he released a long-held and greatly relieved, "Whew! I don't know how you did that, Glory, but I have to hand it to you." With a glance over his shoulder, he invited Sam to share in the admiration. "Come on, Sam, tell the truth now. Have you ever met anyone as multitalented as our Glory?"

Sam wasn't sure what he'd just witnessed, much less that any real talent had been involved. But instead of voicing questions, he gave a noncommittal reply. "That was a fancy bit of footwork, Glory."

She laughed breezily. "Oh, if I'd had to use my feet, we would all be on our way to jail right now."

With a powerful roar, the motorcycle accelerated and flew past the car with Officer Hickman tucked behind the windshield like a jockey.

"Hunny scared him away," Allie pronounced with satisfaction.

"He certainly did." Damon leaned over to pat Glory's cheek with his hand. "With a little help from his garden angel."

Sam wanted to reach between the front seats and toss Damon's hand back where it belonged—which was nowhere near Glory. Instead he pursed his lips and stared pensively out the rear window at the plot of wildflowers and its graceful flock of butterflies.

"I wish I'd asked if I could ride his motorcycle." Glory sighed and popped the stick shift into first. Then, without so much as a glance over her shoulder, she accelerated onto the expressway, shifted gears, and went from zero to seventy in slightly over six seconds.

"I CAN'T BELIEVE IT. We're here on time and Morrison is late." Damon flipped a switch, turning on the conference room lights. "You must have an angel in your pocket, Sam. Usually, you're not so lucky."

"Usually, I have my own car and I don't have to hitch a ride with Romeo's Driving School for Blondes."

"What's with you? You're not mad because I let Glory drive my car, are you?"

Sam opened the hasps of his briefcase with a satisfying snap. "You can put Lassie behind the wheel for all I care."

"Ohh, I see. I am beginning to get the picture on my big-screen TV."

"What are you talking about?"

"Not what. Who." Damon plopped into one of the chairs and put his feet up on the conference table. "We're talking about Glory, your garden angel. Remember?"

Sam placed a stack of papers on the table. "I don't have the patience for this, Damon. By some lucky chance, Morrison is late. Let's spend the time going over the sketches again, not arguing about Allison's nanny."

"Who's arguing? I'm stating flat-out that she's attractive and I'm interested." Damon's pause was sly. "And what's more, I think you're interested, too."

The conference room seemed uncomfortably warm all of a sudden. Sam walked to the thermostat and made a small adjustment. "You don't think Morrison would stand us up, do you?"

"The least you can do is be honest with me, Sam. If you've got your eye on Glory, just say so, and I'll promise not to gloat when she chooses me over you."

Sam eyed Damon with an annoyance that was way out of proportion to the teasing nature of the discussion. "Forget it. She's off-limits and I want you to back off. Glory is Allison's nanny and I don't want her distracted by your fixation on blondes. Got it?"

"Say no more. I'll distract her on her time, not yours. She *will* get a day off now and then, won't she?"

Sam picked up his briefcase and set it aside. His anger was sharp and stinging, all the more so because he had no acceptable explanation for it. The idea that Damon was interested in Glory was disturbing. But not nearly as disturbing as the realization that he, himself, was behaving like a jealous lover. "She'll have time off," he said tightly. "Now, do you think you could concentrate your energy on something slightly more important than your next romantic conquest?"

With a sigh, Damon moved his feet off the table and spread out the blueprints of the old hospital building. "You know, Sam, sometimes I think you buried the best part of yourself with Jenny."

Sam only wished he could deny it.

"GLORY, LOOK! I made a picture of Hunny's tail." Allison held up the sheet of paper. "See? It has spots and everything."

Glory admired the photocopy from every angle. "It's positively stunning. What else can we copy?"

"I know! Let's do his nose!" She squashed the dragon's face against the glass and held down the lid. "Push the button! Push the button!"

Glory pressed Start. A bright white light leaked from beneath the lid, moving from the front of the glass to the back in a whir of automation. As a sheet of paper glided into the tray, Allison grabbed it and waved it in front of the dragon's crumpled face. "We made your picture, Hunny. Look, aren't you stunning?"

"He looks uncomfortable to me," Glory said. "Maybe you should leave the top up next time and give him some breathing room."

"Okay." Allie laid the dragon on the glass again and made several careful adjustments of his position before she pushed the button. The light moved like magic, splashing the room in momentary brilliance. "Did you see that? I think there might be a *star* inside." Her eyes were wide with wonder, her voice brimmed with amazement. "Let's do it again!" Allie gave the starter another jab, but this time when the light came on, she jerked the dragon off the glass and leaned over to watch the movement.

"Doesn't that hurt your eyes?" Glory asked with a blink.

"Hell, no." Allison bent closer to the copy machine and pressed the button again.

When the brilliance was just a couple of black spots in her vision, Glory splayed one of her hands on the glass and pulled the cover down over it. "You know, Allie, some people think hell is a place they would never want to go. And some people think it's like a bad dream that never ends." She nodded at the control panel. "Push the button."

Allie gave the starter an enthusiastic jab.

"But most people," Glory continued, "think hell is a word that shouldn't be spoken by anyone, especially not children. Would you like to know what I think, Allie?"

The child gave a noncommittal shrug.

"I think hell is a word you use to get Sam's attention."

"Sam isn't in here." Allie noted. "He's in the meeting."

Glory sensed that his negotiations weren't going much better than hers with Allie. Riding herd on the cherubs hadn't prepared her for this. Bending down, Glory put her hands on Allison's shoulders. "Let's think of a different word to use when we want attention, shall we?"

"If you want his attention," Allison advised, "you should say 'damn it.' That's Sam's most favwrit word."

"Yes, well, Sam needs to think of some new words, too." She looked into Allie's big bright eyes, hoping to see some sign of comprehension. But the expectant, elfin smile she received in return revealed all too clearly that Allie knew how to handle the adults in her life. "Maybe Hunny can think of a good word," Glory suggested.

"Nope. He only knows bad words and I tell him not to, but he says them and he gets in trouble all the time." Allie sighed loudly and lifted her little shoulders in a what-is-a-mother-to-do kind of shrug before she matter-of-factly picked up the dragon and kissed him on the nose. "But I love him, anyway."

"Of course you do. He's a great dragon." Glory thought it was time to try an alternative approach. "I know a word that would get Sam's attention and wouldn't get you or Hunny in trouble, either." She hesitated, giving the idea room to grow. "Do you want me to tell you the word?"

Allie pressed the starter and watched the light travel across the glass. "I think that really is a star in there. It's brighter than the whole sun!"

"Hmm, that is bright. Don't you want to know the word I thought of to get Sam's attention?"

Allie picked up the copy paper with the imprint of Glory's hand on it. "I want a picture of my hand. But leave the lid up, 'kay? I like to see the star."

Glory reached over and positioned the child's hand on the glass. "Oh, well, if you don't want to know the word I thought of, that's okay. I doubt you'd be able to say it, anyway."

Allison turned contemplative brown eyes on Glory, but all she said was, "I'm ready. Push the button."

Obviously one of them didn't understand the principles of reverse psychology. Glory pushed the button and held down Allison's hand while the star made its smooth, blinding trip under the glass. Maybe a slightly different strategy would work. "You know, Allie, the more I think about that word, the more I know you wouldn't be able to say it."

"I could say it if I wanted to," Allison assured her.

"Oh, I don't think so. You're only five."

"I go to kindergarten next year."

"Yes, I know, but this word is too hard for you."

With an impatient sigh, Allison took the bait. "It won't be too hard. Tell me the word and I'll say it."

"Saying it is the easy part. Using it all the time instead of those other words... well, that's the hard part."

"I can do hard parts, Glory. And I can say hard words."

Glory pressed her advantage. "You won't get mad if you can't say it?"

Allison put her hand on her hip. "I won't get mad because I can say any word I want to."

With a frown, Glory sat on the floor, stretched out her legs, and leaned back against the copy machine while she pretended to consider the matter. "Sam will be surprised when he hears you say this word, Allie. You'll have his attention just like that." She tried to snap her fingers, but they skidded against one another without making a sound. "In fact, it makes me laugh just to think about what he'll say."

"He'll say—" Allie dropped her voice to mimic his low pitch "—'Young lady, where did you hear that word?'" She giggled as she let her feet slide out from under her and she landed—kerplop—next to Glory. "And I'm going to tell him you told me to say it."

"Are you trying to get me in trouble with Sam?" Glory reached over and tickled Allie under the chin. "You wouldn't do that to me, would you?"

"Yes." Allie giggled again as she tucked her chin defensively against her chest. "But I won't really get you in trouble, Glory. I'll just make Sam laugh because he will be so surprised when I say..." She frowned and looked sideways at Glory. "What's the word I'm supposed to say?"

"Daddy."

"Daddy?"

Glory nodded. "Don't you think that's the perfect word to use when you want to get his attention?"

Like an energy-efficient light bulb, the idea flickered and then grew bright in Allie's eyes. Clutching Hunny by the scruff of his scrawny neck, she scrambled to her feet. "I'm going to try it right now."

"Wait. Allie—" But in the precious seconds it took for Glory to maneuver her uncooperative feet into a supporting role, Allison was already out of the room and running down the hall. Glory reached the hall-

way just in time to watch Allie burst into the conference room and yell at the top of her sizable young
lungs...

　"Daddy!"

Chapter Five

"This is my office. We'll talk in here." Sam held the door as Glory moved ahead of him into the room. He glanced over his shoulder at Allison, who now sat at his secretary's desk, busily typing letters under Mrs. Doerner's—and Hunny's—obliging supervision. He closed the door and leaned against it.

Glory faced him, her hands braced behind her on the mahogany edge of his desk, as if she were about to face a firing squad. Not a bad analogy, he thought. Considering the circumstances, not bad at all. Crossing his arms at his chest, he decided it wouldn't hurt to let her sweat for a moment or more.

Not that she appeared particularly concerned. In fact, she looked cool, collected, even a little amused. Another minute of studied silence ought to take care of that, he thought—and then made the mistake of letting his gaze take a lazy descent down the impressive length of her legs. Like an August bonfire, his neglected passions caught the spark of attraction. A fine mist of perspiration moistened the back of his shirt collar, and he forced his eyes up to less treacherous territory as he automatically reached to loosen the knot of his tie.

She watched his actions with an unselfconscious and curious gaze, all wide-eyed with interest, and he wondered what was going through her mind. Whatever it was, he didn't think it was in any way related to the job he'd hired her to do. In fact, he had the most unsettling feeling that she was thinking about *him* in a most personal way, assessing his body as he had just been assessing hers.

"If you don't mind..." He cleared his throat. "Could I have your attention for a moment?"

She lifted her eyes to meet his, and then she did the last thing he had expected under the circumstances—she laughed. "You want my attention?" she asked, and then she laughed some more. "That's good, Sam. Very good and just in time, too. I was beginning to think you'd lost your sense of humor."

He was beginning to think he'd lost his mind. "I'm afraid I don't see much humor in this, Glory."

"You don't?" Her forehead creased with a momentary frown. "Hmm. I thought it was funny because Allie and I were talking about how to get your attention and—"

"You certainly succeeded in getting it, didn't you?" Frustration deepened the gruffness in his voice and her smile disappeared entirely.

"Allie didn't mean to cause a problem."

"Of course, she didn't. And if you'd been doing your job—which *is* to provide her with adequate supervision—she wouldn't have had the opportunity, would she?"

Glory looked down at the plush, teal carpet. "It was only a little disruption, Sam."

He uncrossed his arms and stepped away from the door. "Do you have any idea what that little disruption is going to cost me? Morrison was already hedging on his commitment when he got here this morning. Damon and I almost had him convinced to stick with us, to sign on the proverbial dotted line, until Allie's *little* disruption provided him with an excellent excuse to postpone a final endorsement yet again." Sam combed his fingers through his hair, disheveling it with his frustration. "What the hell were you thinking about, allowing her to run wild in the office like that?"

There was suddenly not a hint of amusement in Glory's pretty blue eyes. "Oh, I don't know, Sam. Maybe I was thinking that a child shouldn't be exposed to coarse language, much less have to use it to gain attention. And maybe I was thinking that you might actually like to hear your daughter call you daddy. Or maybe I happen to think Allison is more important than any meeting could ever be."

"Don't twist this into some psychobabble about a child's need for attention. I am fully conscious of the stress and anxieties that Allison suffers because of her mother's death. But I am also aware that my daughter needs some major doses of structure and discipline in her life. She has been coddled to death already, and I'm not going to allow you to undermine my authority with her. Do you understand?"

"Not a word," Glory said with a shrug. "It doesn't make any sense for you to get upset because she called you daddy."

"That isn't the reason I'm upset. I'm upset because she interrupted the meeting."

"She was excited."

"Yes, I'm aware of that. The problem here, Glory, is that it is your job to keep her from getting so excited."

She studied him for a second. "Excitement? *That*'s the problem?"

He nodded. "In a nutshell."

"You're the nutshell." She straightened and pushed away from the desk. Before Sam had time to blink, she was standing right in front of him, hands on her hips, her gaze duelling with his . . . so close he could feel the heat of her body . . . so close he could smell the cool, airy, heavenly fragrance of her . . . so close he could kiss her on the lips if he bent just a little. . . .

Unexpectedly, she poked his chest with her finger, derailing his train of thought. "Now, you listen to me, Sam Oliver," she began, "I may be only an apprentice angel, but I know a problem when I see it. And if you think *excitement* is the problem, then you need a refresher course on just what life is all about." She gave him another emphatic jab of her finger. "Because I'm here to tell you that if you keep killing the joy in every single moment, you're going to miss out on all the good years you have ahead of you. And if I can't change your perspective on that, I am going to end up sweeping stardust. Do you understand?'' She jabbed him again and then looked at her finger as if she were shocked to see it pointed at him. With a sheepish smile, she tucked the finger under her thumb. ''Sorry about that,'' she said. ''I'm not usually so...physical.''

Sam impulsively reached up and wrapped his hand around her fist. He wanted to deny her charge against him. He wanted to summarily dismiss her and send her, in disgrace, back to the Guardian Angel agency. But more than anything else, he wanted to taste the excitement waiting for him in her kiss. She stared up at him, her expression shifting subtly into one of soft, dewy-eyed anticipation, her lips moist and parted invitingly.

He had no business being so close to her, he thought. A kiss would only complicate everything. *Everything.* And his life was already overflowing with complications. The very last thing he needed was another person to have to think about. The very last thing he wanted was—

''You're in worse shape than I thought,'' she said just before she came up on her tiptoes while pulling down his head with her hand. Their lips met halfway between the joint effort, and the initial touch sent shock waves of exhilaration shooting through his veins. Of their own accord, his arms wrapped around her, drawing her close...closer...shaping her body with his own need.

With a touch of his tongue and a gentle nudge of his lips, he molded her mouth to his...and the sweetness that ricocheted through his body was warm and willing and wonderful. She kissed him freely, with no trace of inhibition or caution, and her arms wound around his neck in an impulsive, oddly stimulating stranglehold.

Holding her was like holding an armful of down pillows, he thought with surprise. She was soft, yet substantial, form-fitting, but resilient, comfortably feminine, but utterly mysterious. And like a favorite bed pillow, she echoed the ins and outs of his body, matching curves to angles in a tempting, tantalizing, but still somehow timid manner.

Glory was a contradiction. While she had initiated the kiss with the finesse of experience, her lips responded to his with unnerving innocence. An innocence that caught him unaware and threw him slightly off balance. He didn't know what to think of her, but he was fully conscious of the emotional power packed in her kiss. Her enjoyment was evident and intoxicating, a tonic for his bruised but beating heart.

He realized abruptly that this was the first time he had ever kissed any woman other than Jenny. She had been his childhood playmate, his best buddy, his first date, his bride. He had loved her so long and in so many forms that their sexuality had grown out of companionship and into a comfortable, satisfying couple-ness. If their relationship had lacked a certain sizzle, he hadn't known or missed it.

At least he hadn't until now.

But the shivery, mercurial sensations skimming through his body like a steamy, summer storm were impossible to ignore. And the pounding of his heartbeat was a fierce and rhythmic fire in his veins. Heat and desire melted together within him as his tongue circled hers in a dance of courtship he'd all but forgotten. And with the pleasure, his conscience awakened to cold, prickly reason.

This wasn't Jenny in his embrace. Glory was a stranger, someone he barely knew. The scorching heat he felt at this moment had to have more to do with the long months of sensual deprivation than with the woman he now held in his arms. His overpowering response to Glory was undoubtedly as simple as raw sexual need. Under the circumstances, any female could have evoked the same reaction. There were times in life when any pair of lips would do, when any warm body was preferable to being alone, when any touch was better than—

Would you shut up and enjoy this? Glory sent the message crashing into his thought waves with a little more force than she'd intended, but she was frustrated that he couldn't just let the kiss exist on its own merit. If all humans were this resistant to pleasure, there'd be no need to worry about overpopulation, that was for sure.

Relax, Sam, it's a kiss, not a complication. She transferred the thought in a softer, more reassuring pattern this time and was relieved to hear his quiet sigh of acceptance and to feel the tightening of his arms as he pulled her closer to him. She relaxed, too, and lost herself in the pleasing art of discovery.

Glory had never thought much about kissing. The custom of pressing one pair of lips against another pair had seemed rather quaint to her until this moment. Certainly, no one in angel school had ever commented on the delights to be experienced in this one particular behavior. But in Sam's kiss she discovered an area of human experience she'd never even considered appealing and yet now understood completely.

Boy, did she understand!

The feel of his lips was soft, warm, and wet. His body was hard and hot against hers. His tongue.... Holy hosanna, she hadn't realized there were so many possibilities. And mixed in with the heat of sexual desire—which she had never in her wildest imaginings expected to flare so quickly—was the unforeseen but very seductive satisfaction of knowing he wanted her, too. No matter how many times he assured himself that he didn't.

She would have liked for the kiss to continue indefinitely, giving her more opportunity to explore the delicious sensations occurring throughout her body. But she'd been warned about overexposure to sensation by angels who talked like they knew, and so, with great reluctance, she drew back, running her tongue over her lips to see if she could taste any lingering magic. "Whew!" she said with a smile. "No wonder kissing is such a popular pastime down here. Is everyone as good at it as you?"

Sam swallowed hard and readjusted the knot of his tie. "I'm afraid I wouldn't know," he said uneasily. "I don't usually go around kissing perfect strangers."

"Who do you kiss then?"

Regret practically swam laps across his expression. His sudden burst of recriminating thoughts met her inquisitive mind and she knew he was preparing to steal every ounce of pleasure from the kiss they'd just shared. "Look, Glory, I should not have allowed that to happen."

She couldn't help but sigh. "Didn't I do it right? Didn't you enjoy it, too?"

"Well . . . yes . . . of course, I did, but . . . Look, enjoyment is not the issue here. I should not have kissed you. Period. You are here to take care of my daughter and nothing—I repeat, *nothing*—is going to happen between you and me to interfere with that assignment. Personal involvement with an employee is a sure road to disaster and, frankly, the only solution I can see is to send you back—"

"Excuse me." She pressed her fingers against his mouth. "Before you go on with this road-to-disaster stuff, could I please say something?"

He seemed to struggle with the request, but finally gave his permission with a nod—for which she thanked him with a dutiful smile. "Kissing you, Sam, is my favorite experience so far, and if you don't mind, I'd like to keep it that way. I promise, the moment I discover an experience I like better, I'll let you know and then we can discuss what a disaster this first kiss really was. Until then, however, it probably will be better for both of us if you stop thinking about kissing me."

Sam opened his mouth but not a sound came out, and Glory decided she should probably make her exit before he found the words he was looking for. "I think I hear Allison calling me," she said, and with a passable two-step, she skirted Sam and headed for the door.

"Wait a minute."

His voice stopped her before she could make good her escape, but she kept her hand on the doorknob as she turned to face him. "Yes, Sam?"

"Just so we understand one another, from this point on you *are* going to give Allie your full attention. Agreed?"

"Don't be silly. Allie always has my full attention."

"Are you asking me to believe that during your 'favorite experience so far' you were thinking about my daughter?"

She shook her head in wonder. "Your life really would be less complicated, Sam, if you'd stop thinking about kissing me."

"I am not thinking about that!"

"Then why do you keep bringing it up?"

"Stop confusing the issue, Glory. We are talking about the job you were hired to do." He covered the distance between them, but stopped shy of getting too close for comfort. "And in all honesty, I don't know why I'm even discussing this with you. I should fire you and be done with it."

"*Fire* me? How do you think you're going to fire me?"

"It's very simple." He pointed behind him at his desk. "I will walk over there, pick up the phone, dial Mrs. Klepperson's office, and ask her to send someone more suitable."

"Someone you wouldn't be tempted to kiss, you mean?" She reached up and playfully tapped her fingertip against his chin. "Forget it, Sam. You didn't hire me and you can't fire me. As hard as it may be for you to come to grips with this, your only choice is to learn to love me."

He stared at her, then turned on his heel, walked to the desk, and picked up the telephone. Receiver in hand, he stood there with a thunderous frown etched across his brow.

Glory took pity on him. "Five-five-five. Two-six-four-five."

He punched in the numbers she'd given and held the phone to his ear. A moment later he hung up. "The line's busy."

"Really? Hmm. Well, keep trying." She opened the door. "You know, Sam. This would be a wonderful day to play in the park. I think Allie and I will go looking for one."

"I don't want you taking Allison anywhere without me," he said in a rush.

"Good. I'll tell Allie you're going with us."

"Wait! I can't do th—"

Glory escaped, leaving Sam to hit Redial.

Again.

And again.

And again....

THE DOOR to the conference room opened just wide enough for Allie to poke her head inside. "Are you 'most ready to go, Dad?"

Sam didn't even bother to look up this time. "Not yet."

"When *are* you goin' be ready, Dad?"

"Soon, Allison."

"In two minutes, Dad?"

He pushed his glasses down and eyed her over the tortoiseshell rims. "Where's Glory? She's supposed to be keeping you entertained."

"She's hidin'." Allie looked behind her, then back at him. "We're playin' hide-and-go-seek."

"That sounds like fun."

"It's not fun, Dad. Hunny is 'posed to be seeking, but he won't 'cause he wants to go to the park right now."

"Hunny will have to wait."

"He'll start cryin'," Allie warned.

Sam pushed his glasses into place and returned his attention to the paperwork. "Close the door, Allie. We'll go to the park when I finish my work."

"*Work, work, work!* I'm *tired* of *work!*" With a sigh of frustration twice her size, she gave the doorknob a jerk, banging the door against the frame. It swung open again, shuddering on its hinges. Allie looked at the door and then at Sam. "I better go find Glory. But I'll come back in two minutes, 'kay, Dad?"

She was off like lightning, her rubber-soled shoes squeaking against the polished tiles as she raced down the hall, leaving the door wide open and the room quiet—except for Damon's soft whistle.

"How did you get her to stop calling you Sam . . . *Dad?*" Damon shuffled a stack of papers and set them aside. "Did you have to bribe her with licorice?"

"She's only doing it to get my attention."

"I never would have guessed."

Sam frowned over the financial data in the hospice file. "I believe the idea was Glory's."

"Ah, Glory." Damon shook his head with wonder. "Now, there's an attention-getter. Gorgeous, smart, and she drives like a maniac. I'll tell you, Sam, she's looking better and better to me every minute."

"Then you'll want to take a long look at her before she leaves the office today. Because as soon as you and I are through revising this proposal, I'm taking her back to the agency."

"I thought you were taking Allie to the park."

"Maybe I will ... after I get rid of the garden angel."

"You're being pretty rough on Glory, aren't you? I mean, it isn't like you can handle Allie all that well yourself."

Sam looked at Damon. "I think I can handle my own daughter just fine, thank you. I certainly have more control over her than Glory seems to have."

Damon shrugged and bent over the papers again. "I can see where it would bother you, knowing that if Allison got to choose, she'd keep Glory and give you to the agency."

"Fortunately, she doesn't get a vote. I'm sure it will make her unhappy for a little while, but by this evening, she'll have forgotten all about Glory."

"I'll bet ten bucks you won't have, though."

"Pay up, big mouth."

"Oh, sure, as if you wouldn't lie through your teeth." Damon stretched lazily, then walked to the credenza and popped the top of a soda can. "You're the only man I know who'd even pretend he wanted to get rid of her. She's perfect."

"She's strange." Sam gave up trying to work and laid down his pencil. "You saw what happened with that policeman this morning."

Damon tipped the soda can against his lips and swallowed. "So she charmed her way out of a speeding ticket. What's strange about that? The woman looks like an angel. Her smile could warm the whole

Antarctic. If I'd been that traffic cop, I wouldn't have given her a ticket, either.''

''No, you would have put her under house arrest.''

Damon lifted an eyebrow in pleasant surprise. ''Very good, Sam. I wish I'd said that. But the sad part is that you, Sam, would have given her the ticket.''

''So sue me for being an equal opportunity kind of guy.'' Sam rubbed the back of his neck. ''It isn't just that one incident, Damon. She says things. And things seem to... happen when she's around.''

''Oh, and heaven forbid that anything unexpected or exciting should happen to you.''

''That is not the point,'' Sam said quickly—before the memory of that unexpected and exciting kiss could skew his perspective. ''I have to consider my daughter's welfare above everything else.''

''Give me a break. Allie is crazy about this woman. I'm crazy about her. She charmed the entire office staff in a matter of minutes. You're the only one who seems to be suffering any doubts.''

''But it's my opinion that counts, isn't it?''

Damon looked at Sam for a long minute before he chugged the rest of the soda and then pitched the can into the trash. ''Fine,'' he said. ''Allie is your daughter and you should do whatever you think is best for her, but you haven't given Glory a fair chance. New employees in this office have at least three months to prove they can handle the job. Even counting the twenty minutes it took for us to drive to the office, you've barely given Glory three hours."

Sam glanced at his watch. Three hours? It seemed longer. Much longer. Scraps of memory flipped through his thoughts, eluding capture as easily as bits of paper in the wind, darting and dancing like butterflies across a field of wildflowers. He pushed away from the table and out of his chair in one cohesive action. "Come on, Damon. Doesn't anything about her seem the least bit strange to you? Her name, for instance. We don't even know her name."

"It's Glory, Sam," Damon said with some concern. "Her name is Glory."

"I was referring to her last name." Sam gave the words an irritable snap. "Do you know what follows Glory?"

"In excelsis Deo?" A droll smile accompanied the phrase along with an apologetic shrug. "You'll recognize that as the only Latin I ever mastered. And I wouldn't know that much if Tanya Freeson hadn't lured me into the glee club just before Christmas our junior year in high school. Boy, do I remember her. Red hair down to her hips. Freckles. Braces. And she wore those gauzy, see-through dresses that—"

"I'm sorry I even mentioned this to you," Sam said irritably. "I just thought you might have noticed something about Glory other than the way she looks."

"Give me some credit, Sam." Damon scratched his chin. "And a little guidance. You're not really getting rid of Glory because you don't remember her last name, are you? I mean, if that's the only problem, I'll go ask her and then you'll know what comes after Glory and we can all relax."

Sam shook his head. "The point I'm trying to make to you, Damon, is that there is something different about her. Something unusual and a little strange. And it's not that I don't remember her last name."

"You're beginning to scare me here, Sam. Obviously you saw or heard her name and forgot it. Or maybe she only goes by the one name. You know, like Cher."

"I would never hire a nanny who didn't have a last name."

"If Madonna applied for the position, I certainly hope you wouldn't turn her down on a minor technicality like that."

Sam didn't know why he'd thought Damon would understand, much less share, his reservations. Though even he had to admit they sounded pretty silly spoken out loud. But still, there was something he couldn't quite remember, a slippery bit of information that stayed just beyond his reach. And until he knew what it was, he couldn't dismiss the confusing idea that Glory was different. Disturbingly different. "Did you notice her clothes?" he asked, hoping somehow to pinpoint the little detail that bothered him. "One minute she was dressed like Eleanor Roosevelt and the next minute, she looked...well, she'd changed her clothes. Her whole appearance, really."

"Something is beginning to seem strange to me, Sam. You." Damon used his index finger to emphasize his point. "Maybe it's a good idea for you to take the rest of the day off. Spend a little time away from the office. Get your mind off Morrison and this hospice project. Because in all honesty, the only thing I consider the least bit strange about Glory is that she seems to prefer your attractions to mine."

"I hardly think that's relevant."

Damon looked offended. "The hell it isn't. Attraction is what this whole discussion is about, Sam. You're attracted to Glory. She's attracted to you. And that, my friend, scares you right down to the soles of your big flat feet."

"I want someone to take care of Allison. I'm not interested in a romantic encounter."

"Then why get rid of Glory? It takes two to cha-cha and if you're not interested, what have you got to worry about?"

"Whee-eee-eeee-eeeeeee!"

Sam caught a glimpse of red streaking past the open doorway. What the hell was Allison doing now, he wondered. A moment later, Glory sailed past, her arms flailing in the air like an awkward acrobat. "Hiiii, Saaaaaaaammmmmm!"

Allison's high-pitched giggle preceded her high-pitched shout. "Glory! Watch out for the—!"

The crash sounded like a dozen bowling balls striking the ground in unison, followed by the slosh and splatter of water, and then a wave of noise, like marbles falling in clusters and bouncing across a tile floor. Sam threw Damon a what-did-I-tell-you look on his way to the door.

With a *snap, crackle,* and a loud *pop,* the electricity went out, leaving the conference room in darkness . . . a thick, black darkness alleviated only by the sunny, sparkling sounds of Allison and Glory's laughter.

Chapter Six

"That was the most fun I ever did, Daddy." Allison planted a sloppy kiss on the side of Sam's mouth before she jumped down from his lap and headed for the slide.

"She is having a wonderful day." Glory cut her gaze sideways to take in her companion's silent and formidable frown. *Smile, Sam!* She sailed the suggestion into his thoughts and got it back so fast the words crunched together in a grumpy *Smam!* With a low sigh, she shifted her position on the concrete picnic bench and tucked her hands under her thighs.

A few feet away in the playground, Allison stood on the top rung of the ladder, lecturing Hunny on safety before she pushed him down the shiny, aluminum slide. She clapped enthusiastically when he landed on his chin in the dirt, then climbed down the ladder to pick him up and begin the procedure all over again. At least Sam's mood wasn't affecting Allie's enjoyment, Glory thought, although she, herself, didn't find much satisfaction in the knowledge. His mood was blacker than it had been before she crash-landed in his back-yard, and Leonard was none too happy with her, either.

"I told you I would fix everything," she said to whichever one might be listening.

Sam turned his head to look at her and the aggravation in his dark eyes stated—quite clearly—his opinion of her offer.

She twisted the toe of her shoe into a clump of dirt. "Mrs. Doerner said she'd always hated that big, old aquarium, anyway."

"I liked that big, old aquarium," Sam said. "It is—*was*—a collector's item."

"We collected almost all the pieces." She tendered a smile, but he didn't accept her offer. "Look on the bright side, Sam. None of the fish died."

"But they're all going to need therapy." A little tension ebbed away and he leaned his back against the edge of the table. Elbows crooked, he rested his arms on the tabletop and watched Allison climb up and down the ladder. "If you don't mind my asking, was it your idea to take the decorative rugs off my office wall and force them into service as skateboards?"

"Magic carpets," Glory corrected.

"What?"

"Skateboards have wheels. Magic carpets glide on thin air."

"So how did my handwoven, one-of-a-kind rugs measure up?"

Glory hunched her shoulders in a wry shrug. "I can't speak for Allie's, but mine sailed across that floor like a pig in bacon grease."

His eyebrows lifted, although the degree of his frown didn't. "Really?" he said. "As slick as that?"

"Oh, much slicker even." She nodded, encouraged by the dry edge of humor in his voice. "It was nearly as fun as when I learned to fly."

"Let's see. That would have been this morning, right after you got behind the wheel of Damon's mid-life crisis, wouldn't it?"

With an inner—and forgivably smug—glee, she sent off a message to Leonard, telling him she was back on track with Sam and that she'd call if she needed further assistance, which she thought most unlikely. "I loved driving that sports car," she said happily. "And I loved skating in the hallway...except for the accident with your aquarium, of course. But I especially love being here in the park with you and Allie." She nodded happily. "Yes, this is my favorite—no, my *second* favorite—experience so far."

Sam's defenses rose like the fur on a cat's back, and Glory realized why *speaking* the truth wasn't always the best policy. Obviously she had to do something quick to keep him from talking about that kiss again. With a burst of enthusiasm, she jumped up and grabbed his hand, giving it a gentle tug. "Show me how to use the swings, Sam."

He resisted her pull, but didn't make much of an effort to disengage his fingers from her grasp. "I'm too old to play on a playground. Let Allie demonstrate.''

''Allie is teaching Hunny to slide down the slide. You'll have to do it.''

''I'm here strictly as an observer.''

''And I'm here to get you back into the swing of things.'' She gave his hand another tug. ''Come on, Sam. Live a little.''

His dark eyes met hers and, in that one instant, Glory discovered that *breathless* was a nervous, excited, exhilarating feeling... and not just a lack of oxygen. ''Oh,'' she said.

''Oh?'' he asked.

''Oh, boy.'' She recovered quickly and shifted her gaze to the swing set. ''I can't wait to swing up high enough to touch those trees. I'm fond of heights, you know.'' She grasped his hand with both of hers. ''Please get up, Sam. It won't take long. I'm a fast learner.''

He moved his hand out of her reach and regarded her with a moment's skeptical, but not unamused, silence. ''You don't fool me for a minute, Glory whatever-your-name-is. I know you believe you can change my mind, but as soon as Allie has had her fill of playing in the park, I'm dropping you at the agency office. The fact that I couldn't find the place earlier only means I should have written down the address instead of thinking I knew where it was located. It does not mean you can stay on as Allison's nanny. You do understand that, don't you?''

"Perfectly. Now will you show me how to swing?"

With a reluctance she knew was more facade than fact, he pushed to his feet and led the way. Eagerly she started after him, only to trip over her still slightly independent feet and be reminded that walking was not as easy as it looked. "Where's a rug when you need one," she muttered under her breath. By the time her cautious steps brought her to the A-frame that held the swings, Sam was already seated in one of the sling straps, his hands wrapped around the heavy linked chain.

"You push off like this—" he demonstrated the technique "—and once you're airborne, it's just a matter of keeping your feet off the ground."

"Keep feet off ground," she repeated. "I should be good at that." Taking hold of the swing next to Sam, she turned around and then checked over her shoulder to gauge the distance between her hips and the U-shaped strip of rubber.

It took a couple of attempts, but she finally managed to control the swing and her feet at the same moment, and she landed in the rubber curve with a plop and a sense of accomplishment. She smiled in triumph at Sam, who swung leisurely back and forth, watching her with a lazy regard. With a firm grip on the chains, she shifted her weight, experimenting with a wiggle and a tightly controlled kick. The swing bounced, but quickly settled back into a dull inertia.

"Put your feet on the ground."

"But you just said to keep them up."

"That's after you get going."

She gave another feeble, ineffective kick. "Can't I get going without using my feet?"

"Only if someone were willing to push you."

"Would you be willing to do that?" She looked at him hopefully...and thought his answering smirk was tacky. "But, Sam, I just got my feet off the ground."

"Well, put them back." His swing slowed with the sheer weight of his frown. "This is not that difficult, Glory."

"It isn't that easy, either."

His lips tightened with impatience. "Look, I don't buy this 'show me how' business. Everyone knows how to swing. This is just another one of those female ploys where you pretend not to know how to do something in order to get attention and play up to the male ego."

She wrinkled her nose and his swing turned upside down, dumping him unceremoniously in the dirt. "You're right, Sam," she said coolly. "And that was an angel ploy to keep you humble."

Without warning, her swing turned traitor and she landed with a *thunk* beside him. Startled at this reversal of fortune, she looked over in time to see him duck as his liberated swing sailed over his head. Too late, she realized the wisdom of his action as the rubber seat of her swing clonked her in the back of the head.

"Ow!" Putting up her hand, she rubbed the sore spot, only to have the silly swing clip her across the knuckles on its next pass. "All right, all right," she grumbled, grabbing the rubber seat before it could chastise her again and wishing, sincerely, that Leonard had taken her at her word and hovered over some other apprentice's shoulder. "That really was not necessary, you know."

"I didn't even touch your swing, Miss Graceful."

"I wasn't talking to you."

"That's good, because if you want to be a swinger, you have to accept responsibility for your own...highs and lows."

Glory turned her head to look at him. "Is that what you call a pun?"

He shrugged. "So I'm out of practice."

"So, practice," she said. The short fall didn't appear to have caused him any injury or even much discomfort. Of course, he didn't appear particularly humbled, either. In fact, sitting there, his feet flat on the ground, his knees bent and providing a place to prop his forearms, he looked relaxed and beautifully arrogant. Or should that be handsomely arrogant? Either way, the dark amusement lurking in his eyes made her breathless all over again.

"You should have told me that *staying* in the swing is the difficult part." She allowed her lips to curve slowly, hoping to bring up his smile along with hers. "Want to try again?"

The shift was barely perceptible, but—yes, there it was—a definite upward slant at the corners of his mouth. "Maybe..." he began slowly, "we'll both be safer if I do the pushing and you do the swinging."

"Oh, that would be wonderful, Sam."

Her smile almost made him forget that she was one disaster after another just waiting to happen. Her simple delight in his offer made him feel magnanimous, made him consider forgiving her for the way she'd manipulated him out of his office and into this park and onto this swing set. He spared a moment's regret for the costly transition and wished she'd managed it without destroying the aquarium, soaking his rugs, and blowing more electrical switches than even the best electrician in town could replace in a day. On the other hand, today he'd heard Allison's laughter, and for that he felt he owed Glory at least the courtesy of a push. "Just for future reference," he said as he levered himself up and off the ground. "Are you covered by a good insurance policy?"

"Only the very best available," she answered brightly.

"All right, then. Put your dusty little backside in that swing again and I'll get you going."

With another ready smile, which was at least as warm as the sunshine beaming down on them, Glory dusted her pant leg with several hearty slaps before she held her hand up for his assistance. "Would you mind giving me a lift up?" she asked. "This isn't my greatest starting position, you know."

Sam stared at her hand, at the delicate smoothness, the intricate shaping, the quiet strength, and knew he was taking quite a risk just in touching her. He ought to have his head examined for being here with her. She wasn't anything like Jenny—and he wasn't anywhere near ready for what he thought she had in mind.

Glory's intent regard crept into his thoughts and he lifted his eyes from her hand to her face. Her beauty struck him with the same sense of admiration he felt for a red-hued sunset or for the silvery assent of the full moon. From tousled gold curls to the dusty brown of her toes, she was flawless, almost mesmerizing in the sheer purity of her face and form. And yet Sam was drawn to her, not by virtue of her physical perfection, but by the utter innocence and serenity he saw in her eyes.

It's all right to risk being happy, Sam.

The words were so softly spoken, he could almost believe they had come straight from her thoughts into his. But the effect was instantaneous, and caution threw a stronghold around his heart. Reaching down, he grasped her hand without ceremony, hauled her to her feet, and released her before he had time to think about the electrifying feel of her skin against his. "Sit down in the swing." The gruffness in his voice was a brusque defense against a siege of tender feelings. "We can't stay at the park all afternoon."

"We can if we want." Glory assessed the swing with a judicious eye before she seized the chains and positioned the seat strap around her hips. "There. I think I'm beginning to get the hang of this."

Oh sure, Sam thought. As if she'd never been in a swing before. As if she didn't know exactly what she was doing to him with her "angel" ploys. "I have work to do this afternoon,'' he said tersely, and took hold of the chains, ignoring the temptation to grasp her around the waist. Even without touching her, though, she was still too close for comfort and he couldn't help but close his eyes against the seductive scent of sunshine and spice that surrounded her—and now him, as well. Damn Damon for ever mentioning the word ''attraction.'' Now Sam couldn't seem to get the idea out of his head.

''We can't stay here much longer.'' With a rough tug on the chains, he pulled her back . . . and back . . . and farther back. ''So enjoy this while you can.'' With that testy suggestion, he released the swing and Glory soared into the air on a gasp of unblemished excitement.

When she swung back to him, he gave her another push, sending her sailing toward the lower branches of a big, old oak that dangled its leaves invitingly close to the swing set.

''Higher,'' she called on the next downward sweep. ''Higher.''

He obliged with another push, and then another, watching her extend her long legs in a valiant attempt to touch her toes to the nearest leaf, feeling his mood lift with her progress, smiling despite himself at her childlike enthusiasm.

''Higher, Sam! I want to touch the sky!''

The sky remained a distant goal, but she came closer each time to the dangling branches . . . almost there, almost within reach. He gave her a last, mighty shove and her toes brushed the leaves into a rustling retreat. Her laughter drifted down around him like a sorcerer's spell, all flash and sparkle, equal parts of music and magic. Maybe, he thought—somehow—this really was her first time in a playground. Or maybe—no somehow about it—he was just a lonely, vulnerable man.

"Oh, Sam," she said in a voice of wonder. "Thank you. This is absolutely my most favor—my *next*-to-most favorite—experience so far."

"Daddy! Daddy! Look at me!"

Sam turned his head to see Allie bowed like a pretzel over the top of the slide, ready to zip down headfirst. He lifted his hand to wave to her and—

Whump!

With a startling thud, Glory's derriere whacked him in the chest, knocking the breath out of his lungs and tossing him off balance. He grabbed her around the waist to keep from falling, but she let go of the chains and Sam tumbled backward, hauling her down with him.

He landed hard in a clump of grass. Glory landed on top of him, compressing his diaphragm and sending what little breath he had left rushing out in a mushy "Whuffffff!"

They lay there for the space of several rapid-fire heartbeats. Him, flat on his back in the grass, and her, flat on her back on top of him. Instead of rolling to one side and off, she relaxed against him and laid her head half on, half off his shoulder. "Now what did you do that for?" she asked.

"Why … did you … let … go of … the … chains?" He gasped for air, but had the presence of mind to note that Glory was considerably lighter in weight than she looked.

"Why did I…" She turned her head, peppering his jaw with the sweet warmth of her breath, making him aware—achingly and unacceptably so—of her body stretched out on top of his. "You pulled me off the swing, Sam."

"Hasta la vista, suckers!" Allison's shout precipitated, by a fraction of a second, her landing on top of Glory, on top of Sam. Her giggles covered a multitude of minor pains that shot through his body like red lines on a road map. As a means of protecting all three of them from injury, he put his arms around the two wiggling females and tried to squeeze them into a less pressing activity. But the moment his fingers touched Allison's side, she doubled up with laughter and began kicking and flopping about like a fish out of water. "Don't tickle, Daddy!" she squealed, even though Sam could barely breathe, much less find the energy to tickle her.

Glory laughed, too, her body stimulating his with a scintillating pressure, her cheek brushing his with tantalizing pleasure. And from some forgotten, neglected corner of his soul, laughter wound its way to his lips, finding voice in a rumbling chuckle, rusty from disuse. "Will you … ladies … get off … me?" he managed to say amid all the giggles and wiggles. But since neither of them made any effort to grant his request, he decided they were fair game and commenced tickling both of them in earnest.

When the jostling got overly rambunctious, Sam took the upper hand and easily wrestled his tormentors to the ground, pinning them, side by side, beneath him. "All right," he said gruffly. "Whose idea was this?"

"Glory's." Allie's smile widened as she shifted the blame, but her bubbly giggle was far from innocent. "She started it. I saw her."

"You started this, Sam," Glory defended herself. "All I wanted to do was swing."

Sam looked from one to the other, taking care not to let his gaze dwell on the flush of awareness in Glory's rosy cheeks. "I think you should be ashamed of yourselves, tackling an old man like me."

"We are 'shamed," Allison said without repentance. "Come on, Glory! Get him!"

Allison's fingers poked into his armpit, but Glory's aim was a little more accurate, unerringly finding the only ticklish point on his body—a sensitive spot just under his chin. He ducked his head, but the laughter escaped anyway, and he rolled onto his back to give it full rein. A sense of release and renewal washed over him, and when Allison jumped him again, he held her tight on the pretext of warding off her attack, but openly adoring every giggly, wiggly, wonderful inch of her.

Glory sat up with a laugh, enjoying the loving that was unfolding right before her eyes. A loving she was miraculously a part of. Bracing her upper body with her arms, Glory leaned back and absorbed the sight of father and daughter immersed in the singular joy of the moment—a moment that plucked at the strings of her own angel heart.

Good work, Glory.

Leonard's praise came unexpectedly—and uninvited. She hadn't been aware of his presence, even though his approval was all around her. She had been so engrossed in Sam and Allie, so involved in their laughter, so intent on their happiness, so...human...for those few moments.

So that was what it felt like. Being human. Being part of a human family. The concepts, known to her since creation, were suddenly and simply real emotions. *I get it,* she said to Leonard. *This is what I was sent here to experience, isn't it?* But Leonard was no longer with her, and she was left on her own to explore the heightened awareness, the infinite flow of emotion that was somehow contained within her physical body.

"Help! Help! He's...ticklin' me...to deff!" Allison's call for assistance was interspersed with high-pitched squeals of delight and Sam's mock pleadings for mercy.

Glory smiled and leaned over to add five more fingers to the game. But she drew back at the last second, recalling abruptly that she was present in their lives as a connector, not a participant. Her assignment was to build a bridge between "what was" and "what is," and then, if necessary, to guide Sam across it. And while her in-body experiences were important in her development from apprentice angel to angel first class, they were incidental to her role as guide and guardian. She was here to protect this family, not become a part of it.

The sting of tears was unfamiliar and Glory blinked them away in confusion. Wait a minute. Crying was not an appropriate response. Happiness and love were the emotions emanating from Sam and Allison. There was no sadness in their laughter, no regret in the game they were playing. The sadness and regret were in her, Glory realized with a twinge of panic.

But she wasn't supposed to *generate* emotion, only hold it for an instant, learn its traits, understand its power. The warnings had been clear and concise. Angels never, ever allowed themselves to get emotionally attached to the humans for whom they were responsible. There were stories—dozens of them—about apprentice angels who lost their heavenly perspective and who never returned from assignment. She had tried, and failed, to think of anything on earth that could entice her to forsake Heaven.

But that, of course, was before Sam and Allison.

"Ohhhhhh...." With an artificial groan, Sam dumped a still giggling five-year-old into Glory's lap and fell back on the grass. "Here, you wrestle her for a minute. Let me catch my breath."

Allie bounced to her feet and balanced her hands on her hips as she stood over her prone papa. "I'll be back," she warned. "And next time I'm bringing Hunny with me." She took off for the slide, going from a standstill to a dead run in the blink of an eye.

This time Sam's groan was genuine and he closed his eyes in exhaustion. "I'm too old for this."

Glory swept an assessing gaze from the tips of his wingtips, up the crease of his trouser leg, over the new grass stains on his white shirt, past the sleeves he'd rolled and cuffed at his elbows, to the unbuttoned opening of the shirt. She nearly reached out to touch the wispy hair just visible there, but knew she didn't dare. The soul-weary lines around his mouth and eyes had eased in the past few minutes, and she was glad to see the change, slight though it was. If she squinched her eyes just so, she could almost see him as he would look a year from now—happy, whole, in love with life and....

She looked away, strangely uncomfortable with the vision. "People get old when they don't stay alive."

He opened his eyes. "Is that what you call a pun?"

"No, just an observation."

A tired frown settled on his lips and he closed his eyes again. "Don't judge too harshly, Glory. Sometimes staying alive isn't the choice. Sometimes it's all a person can do just to keep on breathing."

His pain engulfed her like the heavy scent of roses, and she met it with a rush of empathy and acceptance. Her fingers closed around his, infusing all the comfort and strength at her command. "You should probably take a couple of deep breaths right about now," she suggested, shifting his focus from what he had lost to what still remained. "Because Allie is coming this way... and she's not alone."

Sam raised his head to view the advancing army, his daughter and her motley dragon. "I'll never survive another attack...unless you'd care to join forces with me?"

"I'm afraid I'm only here as an observer."

"Herrrrreeee weeeee coommmmmmmeeeee!" Allie launched the assault by tossing Hunny through the air. He landed in Glory's lap with all the force of a two-pound marshmallow.

"Looks like you've just been recruited, angel," Sam said as he held up his arms for protection. "On guard!"

Allison leapt into the fray, her arms and legs spread-eagled for maximum coverage, and in one brilliant strategic attack, she took Glory and Sam down together.

"GUESS WHAT, DAD?"

"What, Allie?"

"This was the best day I ever did."

"I'm glad you enjoyed yourself."

"I 'joyed you, too. And guess what, Dad?"

"What, Allie?"

"Hunny 'joyed you, too."

"That's good." Sam tucked the quilt around Allie's shoulders, being careful not to cover the dragon's nose. "Why don't we stop talking and let Hunny get some sleep? He looks pretty tired."

"Dragons don't get tired." She rolled her eyes as if everyone knew that.

"Well, daddies do, and your daddy is going to bed." He stood and smiled down at her, still wondering how their relationship had changed so dramatically since this morning. "Good night, Allison."

"Good night. But guess what, Dad?"

"You're tired, too?" he suggested.

She giggled, as if he'd told a funny joke. "I like Glory."

"I know you do."

"You won't make her go away, will you?"

He sighed. "No, Allie. I won't make her go away."

"Not even when you find the age'cy?"

"Not even then," he assured her.

She yawned and gave him a suddenly sleepy smile. "Guess what, Dad?"

"What, Allie?"

"Glory's a real garden angel." Her eyelids drifted down and a soft, drowsy sigh parted her baby lips.

Sam tiptoed to the doorway, turning for a last tender look at his daughter before he drew the door partially shut. In a single day he'd gone from being Sam to being Daddy, from feeling totally inept with parenting to believing there was hope for him after all. He was grateful, and humbled, by the change, and while he couldn't come up with a reasonable explanation for it, he was willing to acknowledge who had brought it about.

Garden angel. He shook his head. What an imagination.

Halfway down the stairs, he heard Glory's voice and wondered, idly, who she might be talking to at this hour. Not that it was any of his business. She was probably on the phone, checking in with family or friends—something she had every right to do, of course. Even if the idea that there were other people in her life seemed somehow, well, impossible.

He cleared the landing and took the last steps in a hurry, anticipating her pleasure when he asked her to stay on as Allison's nanny. He followed the sound of her voice through the study and into the barren rose garden beyond. She was sitting on her heels as if she had just stooped down to pull a weed from the garden path. Her golden curls glinted like stardust in the glow of a huge round moon that hung suspended in the black and silver mosaic of night sky.

Garden angel. At this moment he could almost believe it.

The soles of his shoes made a telltale scrape as he stepped onto the flagstone path, and Glory looked up, smiling at his approach. A ripple of satisfying awareness rolled through him, only to tangle with an elusive dread when he saw the stubby-legged, long-eared, droopy-eyed hound at her feet.

"Look, Sam," she said in perfect delight. "Isn't she the dearest thing you've ever seen?"

He would never have believed a dog could grin... until Ethel's slobbery lips parted in a smirk of canine triumph. "What," he began tersely, "is that four-legged trash hound doing in my yard?"

"She's just getting acquainted with her new surroundings, that's all."

"New— Oh, no. No, she isn't. That's Ethel and she belongs next door." He turned toward the study. "I'll just give her owners a *courtesy* call to let them know she's out."

"They're not home." Glory stroked the dog's long, floppy ears. "They left about ten minutes ago. They'll be gone all summer."

A sense of impending disaster tapped him on the shoulder, and Sam turned to face it head on. "Please tell me you didn't offer to keep that stupi... that mangy mutt while they're gone."

"I knew you wouldn't mind, Sam. Look at her." Glory cupped the dog's muzzle in her hand and smiled into the woebegone, bloodshot eyes. "She's so precious. How could she be a problem?"

"No," he stated with unequivocal passion. "Absolutely, positively, no way is that animal welcome in this house. There are kennels all over this town, and if those idiots next door are too cheap to pay for one, then they deserve to come home and have to pay a hefty fine at the local dog pound."

"Really, Sam." Glory picked Ethel up and crooned softly to the dog as she carried her right past Sam and into the house. "There's no need to get so upset. She's a lovely dog and very well behaved. You won't even know she's in the house."

"That's because she won't *be* in the house. If I have to pay for a kennel, myself, I'm not baby-sitting any basset hound—and especially not that one!"

Glory put the dog down, and Ethel immediately put her nose to the floor and waddled in a tight circle. "For your information, her owners tried to find a kennel to take her to," Glory informed him.

There was a qualifier in there, somewhere, Sam was sure. "They tried, but...?"

"But the kennel wouldn't take her until after the puppies are born."

Disaster froze his vocal chords for an instant while Sam stared at the woman who seemed oblivious to his anger—and to the basset hound who was sniffing suspiciously at the only Oriental rug in the whole house.

"Puppies?" He forced the word from his mouth in a disbelieving squawk. "She's having... puppies?"

"Well, not this minute, but probably soon. Isn't that exciting?" Glory gave Ethel an approving pat before she lifted her own shining eyes to meet Sam's stunned gaze. "You know, Sam, your life is just one little miracle after another."

Chapter Seven

The doorbell tolled out a few tinny, dysfunctional notes, vaguely recognizable as the "Hallelujah Chorus." Sam pulled off his glasses and massaged the bridge of his nose, wondering what he'd find when he checked inside the mechanism. Probably a nest for a once-homeless hummingbird or the temporary living quarters of a family of honeybees. In the past week his home had developed a magnetic attraction for the underdogs of the world. Species was incidental. Size unimportant. No one was turned away. Come one, come all. Make yourself at home. Eat, drink, multiply. It seemed to be common knowledge in the animal kingdom that "Sam wouldn't mind."

A skinny, horse-faced tabby cat, named Dobbin, skittered past the open doorway, his claws scraping frantically at the polished wood floor in an effort to gain a foothold.

"Here, Dobbin! Here, kitty, kitty!" Allison dived past the doorway and slid across the hall on her belly like a baseball player making a dive for home plate. "Come back here, kitty!"

The cat escaped into the study, raced behind Sam's chair, and in a single desperate leap, caught hold of the drapes and climbed to the valance, out of reach.

"I see you, kitty." Allie advanced into the room. "Don't worry, Dad. I won't let Dobbin 'sturb you." With a great deal of scraping and scooting, she pushed a chair under the window. "Com'ere, kitty, kitty."

"Leave the cat alone, Allison."

Oblivious to any purpose but her own, Allie climbed onto the chair cushion and stood on tiptoe, stretching her hand toward the cat's twitching tail. "He wants to play with me, Dad."

The doorbell whined again and Sam pushed back his chair, walked around the desk and, in a one-arm swipe, pulled Allie from the chair. He set her feet on the floor, picked up the chair and put it back in front of the desk. "When the cat is ready to play with you, he'll let you know. For now, though, you should leave him alone."

"But, Dad, we're playin'!"

"Then it's obvious he needs a time-out. You run on and find Glory. I'm sure she'll play with you."

Allie's lower lip jutted out. "She can't wear the doll clothes. And 'sides, she's busy making somethin' in the kitchen."

"Hmm." Sam sniffed the air and remembered that he'd intended to check the batteries of the smoke alarms before Glory stepped foot in the kitchen again.

The doorbell pinged out another summons and he turned toward the doorway.

"There's someone at the door!" Allie bolted past him, headed for the foyer, and Sam wondered why no one else in the house ever seemed to hear the doorbell until he got up to answer it.

Above his head, Dobbin asked for political asylum with a pitiful, "Meow."

"Don't even think about it." He frowned at the cat perched atop the drapery valance. "Just so we understand one another, Horseface, the first opportunity I get . . . you're in a sack and out of here."

The cat twitched its scrawny tail in offended reply, but Sam ignored the challenge, walked to the doorway and stepped into the hall. He was just in time to see Allie slam the front door and plaster herself against it like the heroine in a B movie.

"Allie," Sam said evenly, "who was at the door?"

"Shh!" She put her finger to her lips. "It's the *fuzz*! But I told 'im he'd never take you alive, Dad." And with that unsettling statement, she raced off down the hall, whooping like a siren.

Rapidly composing an apology and the assurance that he would never allow his daughter near another television set, Sam opened the door to a young uniformed officer who introduced himself and verified Sam's identity. "Cute kid," he added without making a dent in his solemn expression. "Which brings me to the reason I'm here. We've been receiving complaints, Mr. Oliver, about your . . . goat."

"WHAT DO YOU MEAN, it followed you home?" Sam demanded. "What are you, Little Bo Peep?"

Glory squinted at the recipe book one more time before she pulled the glasses to the tip of her nose and looked over the thick turquoise rims at Sam's glowering countenance. "I don't know why you're so upset, Sam. She hasn't been a bit of trouble."

He waved the citation like a red flag. "And what do you call this?"

"A speeding ticket?"

"Very funny. The fact is, Glory, it is illegal to keep farm animals in the city limits. This may come as a shock to you, but a goat is a farm animal."

"She's a pygmy goat, Sam. Some people keep them as pets."

"*Some* people keep boa constrictors. But *I* don't want a boa constrictor as a pet. And I don't want a pygmy goat. Or a grouchy cat. Or a pregnant basset hound. Or any of the other strays that you have coaxed across this threshold in the past week. I want them out of here, all of them. Out. Farm animal or not, I want them out. Is that understood?"

"Perfectly. But I have one thing to say to you, Sam."

"And what would that be, Miss Greenjeans?"

Glory pushed the glasses back into place on the bridge of her nose. "E-I...E-I...O."

He had half a mind to kiss that saucy smile from her lips, but fortunately his sensible half held sway and he just stood there looking down at her as she looked up at him. Who did she think she was, anyway? Taking over the household, filling Jenny's spotless house with cat hair and paw prints and whatever it was a goat left behind? Filling his days with frivolous interruptions and his nights with fanciful dreams....

"Wait a minute," he said, suddenly aware of a difference in her appearance. "Where did you get those glasses?"

"The J. C. Penney's catalog. Do you like them? They came with the outfit." She stepped back so he could admire the turquoise shorts and matching shirt. "Sandals, too."

"Very nice," he said. "But do you really need sunglasses in the kitchen?"

"I hope not. But I found this new recipe and...well, considering how the smoke stung my eyes last time, the sunglasses just seemed like a good idea."

"Protective eyewear for the beginning cook. That's very innovative, Glory." Lifting a finger, he touched the first of a series of food splatters that trailed across the front of her shirt in a random pattern. "Most people probably wouldn't have bothered with anything more protective than an apron."

"Did I get something on me?" She tugged loose the hem of her shirt and held out the material so she could check it for stains. "I don't see anything."

Smiling slightly, he put his hands to her temples and lifted off the dark sunglasses. His thumbs just brushed her cheeks in the process—a touch, nothing more than that—and yet he was unprepared for the sensual craving that rushed through him with the contact. He kept a tight hold on the glasses, thinking that it was better to hold any object than to have a pair of empty hands just aching to be filled with her. He wanted to kiss her. He'd been fighting the feeling for days now. Ever since she'd said that kissing him was her favorite experience. Ever since the memory of that one, unexpected kiss had begun cropping up at regular—and irregular—intervals throughout his days.

"I don't know how that happened." She licked her fingers and began rubbing at the stains. "I thought I was being so careful."

He thought he was being careful, too, but the urge to kiss her would not go away. Abruptly, he turned away from temptation to set her sunglasses on the windowsill above the sink. The countertop was a mess and he didn't need to touch it to know it was coated with something sticky. An opaque mixing bowl brimmed to overflowing with a rich, gooey-looking concoction, and on impulse he dipped his finger into it and then stuck the finger in his mouth.

Interesting blend of flavors. Sweet. Surprisingly edible. He nodded in approval and took a second taste. "Hmm. Pretty good, Glory. What is it? No, let me guess. You're making angel's food, right?"

She stopped rubbing at the stains on her shirt and looked up with a frown. "Give me credit for having some imagination, Sam. It's a new recipe I thought you'd want to try. Let's see. It's called a, uh—"

squinting, she bent closer to the open book on the counter "—an aphrodisiac."

He choked. "What?"

"An aphrodisiac. You know, with oranges and coconut? Food of the gods stuff?"

"Ambrosia," he said with noticeable relief. "You mean ambrosia."

Her laughter snuggled up to him like a big, plush teddy bear. "Ambrosia. That's it. I don't know why I get those two things mixed up. One's a dessert and one stimulates the sex dri—"

"I'd better check on Allison." Sam headed for the door, like the coward he was.

"SHE'S REALLY DONE IT this time, Dad."

Allison met Sam at the front door and led him upstairs where Glory was sitting cross-legged in the hall, surrounded by dirt and dust balls, trapped in a corner by a vacuum cleaner that growled every time anyone touched it.

"I don't know what happened. One minute it was working fine, and the next minute it went *clackety-clackety-clack* and dust blew everywhere." Glory lifted her shoulders in a hopeful little shrug. "Do you think you can fix it?"

"Don't touch it, Dad," Allison advised. "I think it might be dangrus."

Sam surveyed the scene for a moment before he turned, walked over to the electrical outlet, and unplugged the cord. The vacuum's angry hum subsided and, with a puff of musty air, the crisis ended.

Allie clapped her hands in celebration. "Yeah! You did it, Dad. You fixed it."

Glory pushed to her feet and dusted herself off. "Thank you, Sam. I didn't know what I was going to do."

"It was nothing." But in his heart, he knew it was a little more than that. Jenny would never have called him out of a meeting with a client, much less have expected him to come home to rescue her. She had been so capable, so much the mistress of the house and everything in it. When she was alive, he'd come home every evening to find the house immaculate, dinner perfectly prepared, and Allison asleep for the night. It was only recently that he'd come to realize it felt good to be a hero—even if he'd done nothing except unplug the vacuum cleaner. "Sounds like you may have swept up something that got wrapped around the beater bar. I'll check it out after I change my clothes."

"You're not going back to the office today?" Glory asked, and he detected a hopeful note in her voice, even though she tried very hard to hide it.

"I think I'd better stick around the house...in case some other appliance runs amok."

"Hey! I've got an idea!" Allie grabbed his hand and held it while she jumped up and down and up and down. "We can all go to the zoo!"

He smiled, always a bit in awe of the way this child made him feel. "I don't think we can afford to take all the appliances to the zoo."

"Dad! Not 'pliances. You and me and Glory and Hunny can go. Isn't that a good idea?"

"I don't think they let dragons in the zoo, Allie. Hunny might frighten the other animals."

"No, he won't, Dad. He'll behave real, real, real good, I promise." The bouncing began again. "Please, Dad, please? I've been wantin' to go and ride the train. And Hunny really wants to see the lizards. Please, Dad? Please, please, please, please, please—?"

"Allison." Glory put her hand on Allie's head and the bouncing became a subdued hop, hop, hop. "I'm sure your father has other things he has to do this afternoon."

"No, he doesn't," Allie stated with authority. "You like to take me to the zoo, don't you, Dad?"

Put like that, he wasn't sure he could refuse. When he caught a glimpse of Glory's face and recognized the eagerness she was trying to contain, he was sure that refusing was the last thing he wanted to do. "What about you, Glory? Would you enjoy a trip to the zoo?"

Her smile grew like a sunflower. "I've never been to the zoo," she said excitedly. "What should I wear?"

"A matching outfit," Sam suggested. "But no zebra stripes or leopard prints. We don't want the animals to think you belong in the cages with them."

Allie slipped her hand into Glory's. "Come on. I'll show you." She tossed a warning look over her shoulder at Sam. "Don't leave without us, Dad."

"I wouldn't dream of it." He stepped aside as they moved past on the way to Allie's bedroom door. "And Glory—?"

She stopped and turned her head, arching her pretty eyebrows in a question.

"Don't forget the sunglasses."

The corners of her mouth lifted. "I'll see if I can find some that match."

He shared her smile for what seemed like a long time as a welcome warmth formed around his heart.

"Come on, Glory." Allie interrupted the moment by tugging impatiently on her garden angel's hand. "Let's get ready before he changes his mind."

"He won't do that." Glory allowed herself to be pulled through the doorway, and Sam stooped down and began winding the vacuum cleaner cord. "Sam?"

He looked up.

Glory was back in the doorway, one hand braced on the door frame, resisting Allie's relentless and unseen pressure to come back inside. "Are you going to let me drive?"

He shook his head. "Not until you learn how to operate the vacuum cleaner."

The slant of her smile changed subtly, and she gave her curly head a toss as she relaxed her hold on the door frame and began to move into the room. "There are some things, Sam, that an angel doesn't need to know."

Crazy, Sam thought. She was going to drive him crazy.

"I'VE NEVER BEEN ice skating before, Dad." Allison watched as Sam laced her skates. "Have you been ice skating before, Glory?"

"No, this is my first time, too." Glory lifted her legs out straight and admired her new foot attire. "I can't wait to get out on the ice."

"Have you ever been ice skating before, Dad?"

"Not in a long time." He pulled his daughter's laces tight and tied the ends in a double bow. "There. Now, we're all set." He looked from Allie's worried frown to Glory's eager smile and thought he must have been out of his mind to agree to this. "Look, maybe I should take you out one at a time and—"

"Oh, don't worry about me." Glory stood, wobbled, and sat down again. "I may need a little assistance getting from here to the rink, but after that, I think I can fly."

"Ice skating isn't as easy as it looks." Sam tried for an upbeat warning. "It takes a lot of lessons and practice to get really good at it."

She turned a reassuring smile on him. "Show Allie how to skate, Sam. I'll be fine on my own."

On my own. His heart made a sharp, immediate protest at the words. He had gotten accustomed to giving her instructions, providing assistance, rushing to her rescue. He liked the idea that she needed him, and he had to struggle now with the impulse to insist that she allow him to help. "All right, if you're sure you'll be okay..."

She met his open-ended statement with another eager look at the skating rink. There wasn't much choice then but to offer her a hand up. He put one arm around her waist and started for the gate that led out onto the ice. She was as unsteady as a newborn foal and he was a little shaky himself. It wasn't the skates, though, that had him off balance, it was his body's instant and insistent response to her nearness. With the slightest encouragement, he would have pulled her into his arms and—right there at the rink entrance, in front of his daughter and anyone else who cared to watch— he would have kissed her until the ice under their feet melted into a steaming hot, huge puddle of water.

But Glory didn't even look at him. She didn't even seem to know he was there as she stared raptly, eagerly, at the few skaters who glided past. "Oh," she said, her voice hushed and wistful. "I really hope this works."

He hadn't so much as released his hold on her arm when she moved free and skated onto the ice like she'd been born with wings attached to her feet. Watching with a strange fascination, he wondered if she'd lied about her expertise to make Allie feel more comfortable. That wasn't like Glory, though. She was honest to a fault. But no one could strap on a pair of ice skates for the first time and ...

Why, it almost looked as if she weren't even touching the ice, as if she were, well . . . flying.

Allison appeared at his elbow, clinging to the rail with both hands. "Did you teach her that, Dad?"

"No, Allie." He couldn't tear his eyes away from Glory's graceful movements, although no one else seemed to be paying any attention to her at all. She was lost in a world of her own and Sam felt lost without her.

Instantly, Glory's feet touched down and slid right out from under her. She landed with a not-so-graceful bump in the center of the rink, reminded by a twinge of discomfort that she was "in-body" and subject to the law of gravity.

You're not here to fly.

Leonard's reminder sent her gaze streaking to the rail, where Sam and Allison watched with concerned and curious faces. She had forgotten for a moment. Forgotten that they couldn't know or understand her actions. She'd seen the skaters and remembered how it felt to have wings. And in her eagerness to fly, she'd forgotten the very reason she was earthbound. *Sorry, Leonard. I guess I got a little homesick.*

Don't worry. Happens to the best of us. His approval and love surrounded her, and then he was gone and she was on her own, again.

Sam reached her just as her knees found a grip on the slippery ice. "Are you all right?" he asked.

"Other than the cramp in my overweening confidence, you mean?" She looked up at him with a laugh. "It is now quite obvious that I do need a few lessons. Can you handle two students at the same time?"

He smiled and extended his hand to help her up. "The more, the merrier, as they say."

She smiled back and put her hand in his, absorbing his warmth, experiencing the tingle of her very physical response, and realizing with a start of pleasant surprise that there was more than one way to fly.

"HEY, DON'T GET MAD at me," Damon's voice on the phone was quick to jump to the defensive. "I'm only telling you what Morrison said. Personally, I'm glad to see you taking my advice for a change and spending a little time on R and R. The business can survive losing a few clients."

Sam rubbed the ache at the back of his neck. Leave it to Damon to give a pat on the back at the same time he was twisting an arm. "I don't see any correlation between my taking a couple of afternoons off and a drop in the level of customer satisfaction. You're still working, aren't you?"

"Well, sure, Sam. But I've never been the hotshot, nose-to-the-grindstone architect you are." Damon's voice had the sound of a complacent shrug. "You know as well as I do that I'm better at PR and you're better at giving the clients what they want."

Sam turned his chair so he could look out at the barren rose garden and the two bright spots of color—Glory and Allison—in its midst. "Considering that I spent most of the past year on another continent, I don't see your point. You obviously managed to keep everyone happy in my absence."

"That was different. I didn't have to deal with hard noses like Mitch Morrison." Damon cleared his throat. "Look, Sam, you're the one who went after him. You're the one who conceived the idea of converting the old Greenwood Hospital building into a cancer hospice in Jenny's memory. And you're the one who persuaded Morrison to provide the major part of the funding. You really can't blame him for wanting to deal directly with you instead of me or someone else in the firm."

Damon was right, of course. Sam had courted the man. He'd wined, dined, and wheedled the funding out of the Morrison Foundation. And he'd chosen to ignore the common knowledge that no matter how benevolent it might appear, Morrison money came with strings attached. "I'll call him," Sam said reluctantly. "Tonight."

"Great." Relief resounded in the single word. "You might want to call Tim Bennett, too. He isn't too happy about the additional rooms and roof angles his wife insisted we incorporate into their house plans. Oh, and Sheila Hutchings wanted to talk to you... I didn't even ask what that was about. And you also might give Johnson a ring, let him explain to you how he managed to screw up the billing on the Ledbetter Office Complex. Oh, and before I forget, Mrs. Doerner is taking vacation starting Monday and you might want to call about getting a temp to fill in for her...."

Outside, Allie jumped up and ran around in a circle, laughing and clapping and trying to coax a doleful Ethel out of Glory's lap. Sam wished Damon hadn't called to remind him of all the people and projects that had a claim on his time and attention. Now, he supposed, he had no choice but to spend the evening taking care of business. Even if he had promised to take the girls out for pizza. Considering that, until the past few days, he'd spent every evening taking care of business, he was a little surprised to feel a genuine disappointment that he had to do so tonight.

"Did you get all that down?" Damon asked. "Do you need the phone numbers, too?"

Allie took a tumble and Sam jumped up, concern taking him the length of the phone cord, but not as far as the French doors. "Uh, no, Damon. I have a phone list here. Thanks."

"Something wrong, Sam? You don't sound like you're paying attention."

Glory helped Allie to her feet and Sam was relieved to see their conspiratorial smiles turning in his direction. "I heard you," he said into the phone. "I'll make the calls."

"Then I can keep my date. Which reminds me, Sam, I signed you up for the Bachelors' Auction next Saturday night. It's a fund-raiser for the Little Lighthouse, so be a sport when they call to confirm and don't argue with my suggested minimum bid of a buck fifty. Take my word for it, you're worth at least that much and, who knows, you might even bring in a buck seventy-five.''

''Don't do me any more favors, Damon. Please.'' And with that, Sam hung up the phone and headed for the garden and his garden angels.

''I'VE EXPLAINED THIS already, Allison. I have to work tonight.''

''But, Dad! You *promised* we could go to Pizza Papa's. You *promised!''* She stomped her foot and folded her arms across her chest. Hunny slouched over one arm, a reflection of Allie's censure glinting in his beady eyes.

''We'll go another time, Allie. Something came up and—''

''*This* is the *worst* day of *my* life! *You* ruined it!'' A teardrop slid past the corner of her eye and she angrily scrubbed it out of existence. ''I'm tellin' Glory!''

She ran from the room, yelling for Glory, and Sam was left with a big ration of guilt and a bigger dose of frustration. How was a father supposed to deal with his child's disappointment? Giving in was out of the question. And he wasn't in the mood to make concessions. In fact, he wished he'd thought of running to Glory for comfort and common sense before Allie had beaten him to it.

Glory had a way of making him feel okay with his choices, all right about his ability to handle life and its resulting ups and downs. He turned toward his desk and the lists of calls he had to make. So, okay, Allie needed comfort at this moment more than he did. She needed a listening ear and a sympathetic heart. He could wait.

Ethel waddled into the study through the open French doors, her belly extended with expectant motherhood and clearing the floor by only a couple of inches. She stopped and looked at him with baleful, brown eyes.

"Don't start on me," he warned. "I already stand accused of ruining my daughter's day. Spoiling your evening would be a snap." He snapped his fingers for emphasis.

Ethel smacked her saggy lips before she waddled past him and headed down the hall to the kitchen. Sam wasn't sure if she was seeking Glory's soothing touch or dinner, but he supposed it didn't matter. Either way, he was the one stuck in the study with his work and a snarling stomach.

Wait a minute. He was hungry. There was food in the kitchen. Could he help it that Glory, Allie, and Ethel were in there, as well? If they were nice to him, he might even order a pizza. Maybe Allie's good humor could be bought for the price of delivery.

"Dad! Dad!" Allie's feet pounded down the hall, and a moment later she rounded the corner of the study doorway and slid to a stop. "Guess what, Dad?" Her ruined day was forgotten, her spirits revived, her smile renewed. Even her seedy-looking dragon appeared happy.

Sam stooped to her level. "Let me guess," he said in a thoughtful voice. "You and Glory think I should order a pizza to be delivered?"

Allie frowned, her momentum temporarily off track. "No, we don't want to order pizza, Dad, 'cause Damon's coming to take us to Pizza Papa's!"

The sudden chill in the study had nothing whatsoever to do with the spring breeze blowing in from outside. "*Damon* is coming here to take us out for pizza . . . tonight?"

"Not you, Dad. Just me and Hunny and Glory." She patted his shoulder. "And you can stay here and work without bein' 'sturbed."

As if it wouldn't '*sturb* him to sit behind that desk, picturing his family out having a high old time without him. "I see." Sam stood. "Do you want Damon to take you to Pizza Papa's, Allison? Is that what you really want?"

Allie tipped her head back and looked him squarely in the eye. "Yes." She clapped her hand over her mouth, her eyes widening with a new line of thought. "I better hurry and get my shoes on 'fore he gets here."

Not a trace of remorse in her whole traitorous little body, Sam thought as he watched her run—of course, she couldn't take the time to walk—from the room and clear the stairs in giant, two-at-a-time jumps. Ethel followed Allison at a slow, one-step-at-a-time pace. Sam turned on his heel and reached for the phone.

Then I can keep my date.

Damon's casual comment now seemed fraught with duplicity. This had all the markings of a setup. Call Sam, get him burdened with guilt for taking a little time off, toss in a few clients who need attention, then slip in and kidnap the women—right out from under Sam's nose. Oh, yes, that was the way they'd worked it. Damon and Glory. Glory and Damon. Damon. Glory. Why couldn't she just have told him that she couldn't survive another minute without a piece of Pizza Papa's pizza? With a righteous anger just about to reach the boiling point, he stalked out of the study and headed for a showdown.

Glory looked up as he entered the kitchen. "Oh, Sam. I'm so glad you're here. I didn't want to interrupt your work, but I... well, I seem to be stuck."

She was standing next to the L of the countertop, dressed in a three-piece, pin-striped suit, as masculine as any attire he'd ever seen on a man, and she was holding the Kitchen King Mixer—the whole, heavy apparatus—in both hands. Her head was bent close to the machine as she glanced down at her dilemma and then lifted her gaze back to him. "My, uh, tie got caught in the beaters."

"How in the..." He hurried to her aid, only to discover he had to pause and take a closer look at the situation before he could do anything to help. The ends of her tie had been caught, then twirled and twisted around the metal blades. The mixer motor groaned with the effort to turn the beaters, while the Windsor knot at Glory's throat held fast.

"I don't know how this happened," she said. "I just turned it on for a minute to see how it worked, but when I leaned across to unplug it, it grabbed my tie and then I couldn't reach the plug and I thought if I picked it up, it would shut off, but now when I try to put it down, it goes faster and—"

"It could have happened to anyone," he said, although he didn't think she believed him. Placing his hands on her shoulders, he pulled her out of the corner toward the sink, until the electrical cord pulled taut and then popped free of the outlet. With a grinding sigh, the Kitchen King died. Sam pushed the release, took the apparatus out of Glory's hands and set it aside, leaving her with only the metal beaters to weight the ends of her tie.

She turned the beaters and pulled at the fabric—and succeeded in meshing the two in a tighter union. With a shake of his head, Sam stepped closer and pushed her hands away. He reached for the Windsor knot and worked until it loosened enough that he could lift the whole tie ensemble up and over her head.

"Thanks." She unfastened the collar button of her tailored white shirt and smoothed the sleeves of her jacket. "It's a good thing you came in here when you did, Sam. Otherwise, I could have been trapped for days."

"I'm sure you would have figured out some sort of solution before the motor burned up. Too bad I didn't get here in time to save your tie from total destruction."

"It's *your* tie, Sam." She offered an apologetic grimace. "I didn't like the one that came with this outfit."

He looked from the tangled mess of metal and the now vaguely recognizable material to the gathering amusement in her eyes and he fought back an answering smile. She looked small and feminine in the typically male outfit. The no-nonsense, starkly masculine cut of the clothes only managed to create an intriguing paradox. He wanted to peel away the layers and discover the woman—but that was not going to happen. She was dressed for her date with Damon and that thought alone summoned a return of Sam's annoyance. "It's too bad Damon couldn't have gotten here in time to rescue you, Glory. I'm sure you'd prefer that he had been the hero."

"Damon?"

"I know what's gone on behind my back. Don't insult my intelligence by pretending you had no knowledge of it."

She bit her bottom lip as she glanced at the mixer on the countertop. "I have an idea of how that appliance works . . . now that I've shared a personal experience with it. But I've shared several personal experiences with you, Sam, and I still don't have the vaguest idea of how your mind works. Could you explain that to me?"

"With pleasure," he said tersely. "I don't like to be manipulated. I don't like to be deceived. And I don't like Pizza Papa's pizza. Now, do you understand?"

She tipped her head to the side and regarded him with bright, unabashedly appraising eyes. "You know, I think I do. Yes. You're tense, frustrated, a trifle quick-tempered and generally out of sorts. And the *reason* you're tense, frustrated, quick-tempered and generally out of sorts is my fault...somehow. Is that right?"

Sam didn't know where she was heading, but her budding smile made him wary. "It isn't *all* your fault."

Her lips completed the curve and she bobbed her head in a satisfied nod. "A textbook case."

"A textbook case of what?"

"Sexual tension, of course." She lifted a fingertip to tap him playfully on the chin. "Luckily, I got an A in that class and I know exactly what needs to happen next. Sam, it's time you and I experienced ...sex."

Chapter Eight

"*Sex?*"

The word developed an extra syllable somewhere between his brain and his mouth, and Sam cleared his throat of an embarrassing adolescent squeak. "You didn't say..."

"Sex." She positioned her fingers at the sides of his mouth. "Say it with me, Sam. Sss-ee-xxx. That's the physical expression of—"

"I *know* what it is, Glory." He caught her instructive fingers in his and, with more reluctance than he cared to admit, he pulled them away from his face. "And you and I are *not* having it."

"But we have all the symptoms."

He ran a finger under his collar—even though his shirt was unbuttoned at the neck. "For heaven's sake, Glory, sex isn't a treatable disease."

"Of course, it's treatable. We just start kissing and—"

"No!" He sucked in a sharp breath, which had no effect other than to make him dizzy. Or maybe she made him dizzy. "No, Glory," he managed in a softer, saner tone. "I don't know where you got your information, but you've got it all wrong."

Her brow furrowed with confusion. "But my instructor was very thorough, and I was curious about this particular aspect of the human condition, so I know I paid attention. And frankly, Sam, I've been looking forward to the experience for a long time."

Sam stared at her. "You're from Mars, aren't you?"

"Don't be silly. Heaven is much closer than that."

Heaven was closer than he could handle at the moment. "But you are an alien or some other kind of extraterrestrial being, aren't you? It has to be that...or else you're just plain crazy."

"You think I'm crazy because I want to have sex with you?"

He backed up to the sink and leaned against it, mainly because his knees were shaking. "Look, Glory, there probably isn't a tactful way to say this but, uh, in this day and age, I find it easier to believe you're from outer space than that you're a virgin who got an A in human sexuality class."

She considered that with a slight frown. "I thought men liked virgins."

Sam closed his eyes for a minute and shifted his weight from one foot to the other and then back again. "I certainly hope your instructor didn't teach that as part of the curriculum."

"I think I read it somewhere. We did once have a class discussion on virgin sacrifice...but that's not the same thing, is it?"

He cleared his throat. "I wouldn't think one would have much to do with the other, no."

Glory moved to his side and leaned against the countertop next to him, crossing her feet at the ankles and her arms at her waist. "You can be honest with me, Sam. Does it bother you that I've never had sex before?"

"It bothers me to be having this conversation." He pushed away from the counter and took a step toward the door. "For one thing, this isn't a suitable topic for us to be discussing. And for another thing... Damn it, there isn't another thing. We are not doing it. We're not discussing it. And we're not doing it."

"Sam?"

He was halfway to the doorway and safety when she turned him around to face her with no better ammunition than the soft, persuasive sound of her voice calling his name. He was a coward. A genuine, dyed-in-the-wool pantywaist.

Sensitive. The word popped into his thoughts like a cork bobbing to the surface of a fishing pond. He didn't know where it had come from, because he wasn't—

Caring. Courageous.

He had the oddest sensation that she knew what was going through his mind, was somehow a part of the battle raging between his head and his heart . . . and a few other sensitive parts of his anatomy. "This can't happen, Glory," he said with a touch of desperation. "It isn't right. You should save the sexual experience for... well, for marriage. Or at least for someone special. Someone you really love."

The tenderness that lifted the corners of her lips touched his rapidly beating heart. And while she stood her ground, not six feet from him, he was losing ground with every heartbeat. In self-defense, he hauled out the heavy emotional artillery. "You should wait until you love someone... as much as I loved Jenny."

Glory didn't even flinch. "Let me try to explain this to you. The sexual experience, if it happens between us, will occur within a—" she gestured with her hands, palms up, as if she were having to search for the right words "—within a different context."

"The context of your imagination?"

She raised an eyebrow. "Or yours. Now, pay attention, please, you may find this illuminating."

"Illuminating? Give it up, Glory. Do you honestly believe you can tell me anything about the birds and the bees that I don't already know?"

Her chin came up. "Talk is cheap, Sam. I can show you things you never even dreamed of."

He was in trouble here—and he knew it. Her eyes, her expression, her posture, everything about her spelled it out for him. She was innocence and seduction, but he'd be damned if he knew where one left off and the other began. She was living proof that temptation came in all kinds of wrappers. Standing there in her men's clothing, she looked more beguiling than anything he'd ever seen in a three-piece suit. "Where did you get that outfit?" he asked, deliberately casual. "The Brooks Brothers' catalog?"

"Oh, what difference does it make? Obviously you've made up your mind and you're not going to listen to me."

"Obviously," he said pointedly, "I want to talk about something else."

"That isn't necessary." She jammed her hands into her trouser pockets. "I get the message, Sam. You've made it very clear you're not interested in having sex with me. You don't have to stand here making chitchat to make me feel better."

Against his better judgment, he stepped closer and stopped in front of her. "I didn't say I wasn't interested, Glory. I said it couldn't happen."

She dropped her gaze. "Forget I mentioned it, Sam. Really. It was just an option. I was probably supposed to wait for you to bring it up, anyway."

Bringing it up wasn't the problem. But she didn't seem aware of her double entendre and he, certainly, had no intention of explaining it. He just stood there, watching her fingers work nervously at her vest, buttoning and unbuttoning the middle button.

"Honestly, Sam, just forget it. That's what I'm going to do. I don't have to have this experience with you. There's no reason I should have allowed myself to want..."

Her voice trailed off into abject silence and he reached out to her, lifting her chin with a touch of one finger. Her lashes lay against her cheeks like wisps of smoke against a sunlit cloud, hiding her soul from his questioning gaze. "What..." he began softly, "do you want? Me?"

With the barest of nods, she raised her eyes to meet his—and the fight went out of him. Her lips were moist and slightly parted, her breath a warm invitation, her expression one of waiting and wanting. And he was, after all, only a man. Bending his head, he brought his lips to hers and with the first touch, the first tantalizing pressure, he wondered what he'd been fighting.

Glory was no threat to him. She was warm, willing...and she was here. It would be wrong to take advantage of her innocence, wrong to even consider her offer. But surely a kiss wouldn't damn him for eternity. Just a moment, a few harmless minutes, to remind him that he was still very much alive. And it wasn't as if the pleasure was all for him. Her lips were full and responsive beneath his, her enjoyment self-evident at every point her body touched his.

She pushed her hands up and over his chest, leaving a mark of warmth and wanting wherever she touched. Her thumbs stroked the hollows of his shoulders, igniting delightful sensations under his skin. His most coherent thought was that if she let go, he would float up and up forever. In response, he pulled her into his arms, holding her tightly against the possibility that she could be left behind.

The feel of her in his arms was strangely elusive, but the vitality in her lips was heart-stoppingly real. He had the conflicting perceptions of a dream—fantasy linked to fact by a series of quicksilver impressions. But Glory was no dream. And the desire that traversed her body to be reborn in his was no illusion. He hadn't thought he could feel this way, hadn't believed his heart would ever even consider putting anyone else in or even near Jenny's place. And now, suddenly, the possibility was flowing through him, flowing from the woman he held and into his thoughts, gaining credibility, becoming a viable idea, forming a hesitant but hungry wish.

Somewhere, in a distant galaxy, he heard music. The round lush notes of a bell chiming a heavenly chorus.

She pulled away from his kiss, wide-eyed and breathless. "I heard angels singing," she said.

"What a coincidence. So did I." He bent toward her lips for a second time, taking them with a demanding kiss, enjoying the eagerness of her response. His hand slipped inside her jacket to caress the smooth, weighty curve of her breast. The vest was in the way. The shirt, too, and he moved his fingers to the buttons that blocked—

"Daddy! Daddy! Daddy! Daddy!" Allie's yelps, accompanied by her thunderous descent of the stairs, were as effective as ice water.

Sam jerked his lips from Glory's like a man possessed, recalling his priorities in a sudden, complete panic. For one tense moment he froze, sorting through a horrifying list of possible accidents and dangers. Then he turned on his heel, moving quickly, purposefully, across the kitchen to meet Allison in the doorway and scoop her safely into his arms. "Sweetheart, what's wrong?"

"Daddy! Daddy! Daddy!" She looped her arms and legs around Sam, then leaned back to look him right in the face. Her eyes were wide with... excitement? Wait a minute. He was having a heart attack and she was merely excited? "Guess what, Daddy?"

"You scared me half to death, Allison." Sam took a deep breath in an effort to calm the frantic pounding of his heart. "What are you yelling about?"

"It's Ethel! She gots a puppy! Anyway, I think it's a puppy! She was wiggling all over the bed and it's all messy and yucky and—"

"Where?" Sam spoke sharply. "Where is she?"

"She's in your room, Daddy. On your bed."

Perfect. He rounded the stairwell and took the steps two at a time with Allie in his arms and Glory following close on his heels. The doorbell chimed in with a summons, but no one stopped to answer it.

Damon opened the front door and stuck his head around in time to see the disappearing parade. "Hey," he called. "Where's the fire?"

Muttering under his breath, Sam reached the up-stairs hall and set Allie's feet on the floor. She ran ahead, entering his bedroom first, halting squarely in the doorway, her hands planted on the door frame. First Sam, then Glory, then Damon dominoed to a stop behind her.

"Sssshhhh!" She warned them. "Don't 'sturb her."

"What's happening?" Damon asked, stretching to see over Sam's shoulder.

"A mess," Sam answered.

"A miracle," Glory corrected.

"Looks like two of them, so far," Sam said with a disgusted shake of his head. "Allison, do you know how that short, stubby-legged dog got on top of my bed?"

Allie flashed an unrepentant smile over her shoulder. "It was a mir'cle, Dad. She jumped."

"THREE, FOUR, FIVE." Allie counted heads for the eleventh time, leaning over the cardboard box to ex-amine the new additions to the household. "Five baby mir'cles," she said with satisfaction. "One, two, three, four, five."

Sam slipped his arm under her and scooped her away from the box. "Allison, leave the puppies alone. Ethel needs to rest and so do you. It is way past your bedtime."

"Is not."

"Well, then, it's past mine and, if I have to go to bed, so do you."

"But this is a special night, Dad. We had puppies!"

As if he could forget. "We're going to have them for a while, Allie. We can't find homes for them until they're eight weeks old."

"We don't have to find homes," she said in a voice that dared him to deny it. "They have the best home here."

"And you have the best nest." He tossed her over his shoulder and she giggled as he closed the door of the basset family nursery—formerly the laundry room—and carried her upstairs to bed.

Glory was turning back the covers as they entered, and Sam caught his breath at the sight of her. It was her presence in Allie's room, seeing her perform the familiar ritual of bedtime that caused his startled awareness, that shackled the rhythm of his heartbeat. At least, he told himself, it was nothing more than that.

Smiling, Glory held out her arms to Allie, who didn't hesitate to change affiliations. "There's five puppies," she said to Glory. "I counted 'em and there's five. Five mir'cles."

"Six." Glory tapped Allie on the nose. "You're a miracle, too."

"And Hunny's a mir'cle, three." She wiggled happily in Glory's arms. "And Daddy's mir'cle four and . . ." Her eyes widened with inspiration. "I know what! We can name the puppies Mir'cle. Mir'cle One, Mir'cle Two, Mir'cle Three, Mir'cle Four—"

"And Murkle Five." Sam mimicked her mispronunciation as he grabbed her bare foot and waggled her toes. "This little murkle went to market.... And this little murkle stayed home..."

She laughed and kicked to get free. "Stop that, Daddy. Stop! It's piggies! Not mir'cles!"

"Oh. I thought I was counting toes." He pulled up her foot and addressed her toes. "Excuse me, piggies."

"You're silly, Dad." Her cupid's bow mouth formed a smile of sweet exasperation, which followed her all the way down to the bed as Glory settled her in for the night.

"He really enjoys teasing you." Glory tucked the covers under Allie's and Hunny's chins, then smoothed away the wrinkles so tenderly that Sam's heart hurt just a little. "Is that because he loves you?"

Snuggling under the covers next to Hunny, Allie nodded happily. "Guess what, Glory?"

"What, Allie?"

"Hunny wants you to stay forever and ever."

Glory's hand stilled and then withdrew across the blanket. "That's a nice thought." She made a show of tucking the loose edges under the mattress, but Sam saw the quiver of emotion at the corner of her mouth.

"And guess what?" Allie directed this stalling tactic at Sam, but didn't wait for his answer. "I think you and Glory should get married and then we can have five girls like me."

Sam's gaze moved quickly to Glory, automatically searching for her reaction, but she didn't look anywhere near him, just kept her head bent, her expression hidden. He was a little surprised to discover that his heart hadn't cramped in protest. It kept beating steadily, and the protest somehow never materialized. "Five girls?" Sam pulled his attention back to Allison. "Why not five boys?"

"Boys eat worms."

Glory moved quietly away from the bed to the window and stood looking out. The moon was too far past the pitch of the roof and couldn't be seen, but its silvery light flowed over her like a gossamer wedding veil. She was breathtaking and it was difficult to look anywhere else, but Sam managed to keep her in his peripheral vision as he absently patted Allie's hand. "I'm a boy."

"You're not a boy. You're a daddy."

"What makes you think daddies don't eat worms?"

"'Cause they just don't." She turned her head on the pillow. "Do they, Glory?"

"Birds eat worms." Glory kept her face turned toward the moonlit sky. "And bees make honey."

"And Hunny is getting very, very sleepy." Sam put his finger to his lips and tiptoed away from the bed.

"Dad?" Allie called softly. "What do worms taste like?"

"Liverwurst."

She wrinkled her nose and Sam took the opportunity to point at the dragon and whisper, "I think he's asleep."

Allie checked and then put her finger to her lips. "Sssshhh."

With a solemn nod, Sam tiptoed to the window and touched Glory on the arm.

She turned, clearly startled, and he wondered what thoughts had taken her so far away. "Sssshhh." He put his fingers to his lips and took her hand, intending to lead her from the room. At the first touch, he froze.

Her skin was on fire, but the sensation that seared through him was energy. Pure, raw, and radiant. Blinding and binding. He couldn't move. He couldn't have dropped his hand from hers if he'd tried. So he stood—forever it seemed—caught in an energy force he didn't understand, held by the yearning he saw so clearly in her eyes.

Marriage. Children.

The thoughts were separate parts of the other, woven together into a panoply of possibilities. Allie had posed the question. Glory offered the answer. But somewhere in between, Sam hesitated, unsure if he had the courage to fall in love again.

With a drowsy sigh, Allison turned on her side, already dropping off to sleep.

"Good night, Allie." Glory's whisper barely ruffled the quiet in the room, but it signaled an abrupt return of normalcy. Sam blinked and looked through the window. Same old moon, he thought. Same stars, same sky. But something unusual had happened just now. He might have imagined the intense surge of energy, but not that haunting, wistful look on Glory's face. He looked down at her hand, still tucked in his. There was still a touch of fire in her skin, a lingering aura of warmth and light. He had a sense of things unseen, a soft stirring inside him. But as she turned to him with a questioning smile, he felt the pinch of doubt, followed by a self-deprecating scoff at his imagination.

He released her hand and cleared his throat, intending to dispel the mood with a joking comment, but all he managed was a husky, "Glory?"

"Ssshhh." She put her finger to her lips, then turned and walked quietly from the room.

He moved to follow her, but caught himself and stopped short half in, half out of the doorway. Standing there, unable to go forward, he thought about Glory and the possibility that he might be falling a little in love with her. Then he knelt beside Allison's bed and, as he watched her shoulders rise and fall in sleep, he made himself remember Jenny.

"I UNDERSTAND, LEONARD." Glory paced through the rose garden, stopping to pull a weed here, a thistle there. "It's not like I planned for this to happen, you know."

Another weed was yanked out by the roots and tossed aside. "Well, it surprised me, too."

She sighed and stopped pacing. "I'm aware of the danger, Leonard. I know what can happen in this kind of emotional involvement...."

Kneeling on the cobbled path, she began weeding in earnest, venting her agitation on the neglected garden. "And I was *so* paying attention in class. There's no need to lecture me. I knew the risk when I took the assignment."

But she hadn't known. Not really. How could an apprentice angel understand the temptation to be a mother, a wife? How could she have even guessed that love would feel so differently from the human side of the equation?

So, what do I do now, Leonard?

It was a request, an honest plea for assistance. And it went unanswered, like a call for help echoing into an endless silence. Sitting back on her heels, Glory surveyed the garden. Not a bloom in sight. Not even a hint of a leaf. It wouldn't take much—a thought, a touch—and the garden would flower into fragrant life. She was an angel. What could be simpler?

Falling in love with Sam? Could anything be simpler—or more complicated—than that?

Glory sighed and dusted off her hands. "You're a big help," she said to Leonard, even though she knew he was gone. "Popping up just long enough to point out my mistakes before dashing off to choir practice as if..."

She looked over her shoulder at the open French doors, sensing Sam's presence in the study. Music curled into the air like the scent of roses, faint but growing steadily stronger. So lovely were the notes that Glory closed her eyes to listen. Even so, she knew the instant Sam moved into the garden, felt his sadness penetrate all the way to the bottom of the heart she had only borrowed.

"What are you doing out here?" he asked.

"Weeding the garden."

"You're wasting your time."

She looked at the barren plants. "I think there's a good chance they'll make a comeback."

"The rosebushes are dead, Glory. What difference does it make if the weeds take over?"

She reached out to show him the difference, her fingers hovering over the nearest plant. It would be so simple. One touch and the chain reaction would begin. Life would rush through the garden like prayers toward Heaven. The rosebushes would stretch, bloom, and unfold their promise in a mosaic of rich color and delicate fragrance. Just a touch of her fingertip and the weeds would give way to a miracle.

"Don't touch it."

Startled, she withdrew her hand and looked to Sam for explanation.

He shrugged. "The thorns are still there. You could prick your finger."

As his loneliness pricked her spirit? She sighed and pushed to her feet. It was probably best that he'd stopped her, anyway. It was her job to open his eyes to the miracles in his life, not create them.

"What a beautiful garden Jenny left for you," Glory said quietly.

"Yeah." His voice was heavy with sarcasm. "Beautiful."

"Sometimes you have to look with your heart, Sam."

"Thanks for that bit of maudlin philosophy. I'm sure that will solve all my problems."

"What problems?"

"My point exactly." He turned to her with a narrowed gaze. "You don't know what kind of problems I might have, Glory, so don't spout off any more silly platitudes. Save the Pollyanna clichés for your next assignment."

She matched his frown, furrow for furrow. "At this rate, I won't get any more assignments. Someone should have warned me how pigheaded you can be."

"Well, someone should have warned me that you take a cockeyed view of every situation."

"Oh, yeah? Well, someone should have warned me that you can't see the trees in the forest!"

"Is that so? Well..." He stopped to correct her. "You meant to say, can't see the forest for the trees."

"No, I meant to say you're pigheaded and you can't see straight."

"Are you trying to start an argument?"

"You started it. I'm just trying to keep up."

He pursed his lips, but she could tell he was only trying to look angry. "This isn't a contest, Glory. You said something irritating and I let you know about it. You didn't have to take it any further."

"Easy for you to say. You had the last word."

"I didn't get to keep it long."

"That's because I'm quick on the trigger and I know more clichés than you can shake a stick at." She looped her thumbs through her belt loops and nailed him with a swaggering smile. "Don't mess with Texas."

His sadness had vanished and his frown followed suit—although he did hold on to it until the last possible moment. When it was completely gone, he surrendered a sigh of laughter. "I think I've been had."

"Not yet. But I'm working on it."

"Are all the nannies at the Guardian Angel agency as sassy as you?

"I keep telling you, Sam. I'm not a nanny. I'm an angel."

He turned toward the study with a laugh. "And I'm a cowboy. Come on, angel, let's go inside. I'll fix you a sarsaparilla on the rocks."

"Is that anything like an aphrodisiac?"

"More like a nightcap."

Glory followed him, glad she hadn't set the garden abloom. Flirting had turned out to be a more satisfying miracle . . . and a lot more fun.

Chapter Nine

"But, Daa-aaad, I want to go with you. I don't want to stay home with Glory." Allison marched out of the adjacent bathroom and over to the closet.

Sam heard the militant stamp of her foot, but he kept his back to her as he continued to search for his missing dress shoe. He was running late. Damon was already on his way. "I know if I don't pick you up, you'll find some excuse not to go," Damon had said. "It's a charity auction and it won't hurt you to socialize for a few hours. You're getting worse about avoiding contact with other people and this time I intend to make sure you do your fair share...even if I have to hold your hand through the whole evening."

Sam had protested, but it was too little, too late. So now he was committed, frustrated, and a perfect target for the guilt Allie was laying on thick. She had been at his heels all evening, talking a mile a minute, observing him with avid curiosity as he shaved, combed his hair, brushed his teeth. It was only when he'd told her she wasn't going that she'd turned surly.

"I wanna go to the oxshun with you, Dad."

He didn't know where she got her stubbornness. "I'm sorry," he said as his fingers located the mate to his shoe. He dug it out from beneath the stack of winter sweaters he'd meant to store. The closet needed cleaning in the worst way. He examined the crowded clothes racks and the jumble of miscellaneous items on the shelves as he balanced on one foot and slipped on the prodigal shoe. Without turning around, he stooped to tie the laces. "I told you, Allie, this is a party for grown-ups. You wouldn't like being the only little girl there."

"I would, toooo—choooo...." Her sneeze punctuated the statement, and Sam felt something hit his back. He grimaced and turned around to see his daughter in the doorway, the lower half of her face covered in shaving cream.

"Did you decide you needed a shave, Allie?"

She wiped the back of her hand across her nose, splattering foam like spray paint. "I want to go to the oxshun," she repeated.

With an impatient sigh, Sam stood and took her hand. He led her back to the bathroom, lifted her up, and sat her on the counter beside the sink. "Don't move," he said, and backed to the doorway. "Glory! I need your assistance up here!"

"She's busy," Allie informed him.

"Glory!" He raised his voice. "Could you come up here, please?"

"Just a...minute!" Her response sounded far-away. In the kitchen, maybe. Probably had her pant leg caught in the Devil Duster or something.

Sam decided there was no way now he could avoid being late. He'd just have to take the time to get Allie cleaned up. He stepped back and started to shrug off his black tuxedo jacket, thinking he could at least save it from further spotting. Allie fidgeted and he raised his eyebrows. "Be still."

She was...for about three seconds. Then she began to swing her feet, not so vigorously that she was in danger of falling, but enough to tweak Sam's annoyance. He forgot about removing the jacket and reached into the cabinet for a washcloth, which he then held under the tap until it was saturated with warm water. "Do you think you can sit still long enough for me to clean your face?"

She exaggerated her answering nod, bringing her chin to her chest and spreading the shaving cream onto the pretty lace collar of her blouse.

With a frown, Sam put the washcloth to her face.

"Ow! You got it in my eye! Ow! Ow! Ow!"

He tamped down his frustration and tried to remedy the mistake, only to have her push his hands away so she could rub her eyes and make everything ten times worse.

"Ow!" She yelled. "Ow! Ow! Ow!"

"Stop yelling, Allie, and let me look at it."

"But it hurts!"

"I know that, but if you'll just let me—"

"What happened?" Glory's voice was calm, soothing, and held just the right amount of sympathy to quiet the child and irritate the man.

"He got soap in my eye."

"I was trying to wash her face." Sam stepped back, ready to let Glory—or anyone else, for that matter—deal with his daughter. "She's smeared shaving cream everywhere. It's on my jacket and I'm going to have to spot clean the thing before Damon gets here. I can't go out looking like a Dalmatian."

Allie sneezed again and a big blob of shaving cream splattered onto his crisp, white shirt. Sam looked down in dismay.

And Glory *laughed.*

He couldn't believe it, but a single glance confirmed it. She was laughing behind the hand she'd clamped over her mouth. He heard a giggle and turned his head to see that Allison—her burning eyes miraculously better—was laughing, too. "I don't see anything funny about this," he said.

Glory gulped down a second wave of amusement, but it came right back in the smile she tried valiantly to hold down. "You're absolutely right." A hiccup of merriment punctuated the words, and her sense of the ridiculous sparkled like a diamond in her pretty blue eyes. "But I can fix that if you'll just stay right there. Don't move, now..." Holding up her hand, she pushed at the air while she backed out of the doorway, leaving him with a Stay command as if she were training a puppy. "Stay...stay..."

Allie's giggles dwindled when Glory left and Sam eyed her with an edge of exasperation that unerringly turned inward. He hated losing patience with her. After all, she hadn't meant any harm. Imitation was supposed to be the sincerest form of flattery.

She lifted her chin and offered a timid smile against a backdrop of foamy white. All right, so he was a sap for a girl who smelled like Old Spice.

"Funny face." He touched her nose and then his own. By the time he heard Glory's footsteps in the bedroom, his face was dotted with shaving cream and Allison was giggling with delight.

"All right," Glory said from the doorway.

Sam turned with a smile...just in time to be blinded by the camera flash as Glory snapped his picture.

"TOO BAD you couldn't wear the tux." Damon tugged on the points of his safari print vest and adjusted the crisp white cuffs just visible beneath the jungle green tuxedo jacket. "The guys wearing tuxes generally bring the bigger bucks. I hope those casual slacks and that sport shirt won't hurt your overall bid by too much. Personally, I would have put on a tie, but then we can't all bring top dollar, can we?"

Sam listened as he surveyed the mostly female audience from the wings of the makeshift stage. "I can't help wondering how much that woman in the front row would bid for you if you'd worn the loincloth instead of the Tarzan formal wear."

Damon grinned and fingered the ends of his bow tie. "If you see her bidding for me, I want you to excuse yourself and start a fire in the men's room. I'm serious. I may be up for sale, but I'm not desperate. Just between you and me, that woman looks a lot like a monkey."

"Then the two of you have something in common."

A round of applause and laughter ricocheted backstage to where Sam, Damon, and several other charity bachelors awaited their turn on the auction block. The sleekly coiffured woman at the podium called the next group of six onto the stage platform by crooking her finger and saying, "Come on up to my place, fellas. Don't be shy."

"That's us. Let's go." Damon made a last adjustment to his bow tie, knocking it slightly askew—an angle Sam thought appropriate for the occasion.

Once on stage, they took turns walking down the runway and back while the bidders politely inspected the merchandise. Not up close, of course. This was a fund-raiser and the crowd was suitably urbane, although one or two women—especially the one in the front row—demonstrated an occasional, and rather tacky, lack of restraint.

"Look at the cute butt on that one," the bold woman in the front row said as Damon made a sweeping turn and walked back up the runway.

"If she bids on me, I'm faking a heart attack," Damon leaned close to whisper.

"Get ready for it," Sam whispered back. "She is going to own you tonight."

Damon's groan was lost in the announcer's call. "We're ready for you, bachelor number seven."

With a cocky swagger, Damon stepped forward and struck a devil-may-care pose.

"Check your programs, ladies," the auctioneer said. "This is Damon Field. Age...?" She looked at the audience and grinned. "He says he'll be any age you want. Profession? By day, he's a partner in the architectural firm of Oliver Field. But by night he's—and I'm quoting verbatim from his bio here, ladies—he's *Fantasy Guy,* the man of your dreams!"

A ripple of laughter greeted this, along with a raucous "Whoo, whoo, whoo" from the woman in the front row. The auctioneer tapped her gavel on the podium and returned to reading bachelor number seven's selling points. "His favorite color is..." She gave Damon the once-over. "I'd say green. Favorite romantic song?" With a lift of her brow, she looked at the audience and said deadpan, "'Dream Lover,' of course."

"It's 'Heaven Tonight' for you and me, Sugar!" yelled the woman in the front row.

The auctioneer turned to Damon with a this-is-for-a-good-cause smile. "I'm tempted to bid on you myself," she said, and blew him a kiss before she banged the gavel on the podium. "All right, bidders, let's do it with Mr. Fantasy Guy. Who'll start the bidding at one hundred dollars?"

Front Row held up her finger and the race was on. Five minutes and a final bid of three hundred, thirty-one dollars and sixty-four cents later, Damon was sold to the woman in the front row. He clapped a hand over his heart and grabbed his throat with the other hand— a dying gesture made for Sam's entertainment—before the winner claimed her prize and led him offstage.

"Bachelor number eight," the auctioneer called, and Sam marshaled his courage to step forward, wondering what he was doing on this stage, in front of all these women, offering his privacy for their entertainment. Why hadn't he just written a check to the charity? He didn't need the humiliation of being bought—no matter how worthy the cause. And he didn't want to spend the evening with a stranger. He wanted to be home with Glory. And Allison, too, of course.

"Just between us, ladies, this bachelor is an undervalued offering." The auctioneer spoke directly into the microphone, lending the words a husky, secretive quality as they went out across the ballroom of the Adam's Mark Hotel. "Sam Oliver, as some of you know, is a new name on the eligible bachelor list. He's the other half of the Oliver Field partnership, but don't make the mistake of calling him Fantasy Guy. You can think it all you like, whisper it among yourselves, but bachelor number eight is the stuff of serious fantasy, and you'll want to handle him with kid gloves. Tonight could be the start of something wonderful for one of you lucky gals. Take my word for it, you don't want to let this one get away. Now, who'll start the bidding?''

Sam's throat closed with her tactless remarks, and he wished there was a way to fake a heart attack and get off this stage and away from this place. But the ritual was already under way and he had no place to run.

He focused his energy on staying calm. When the bidding was over, he'd tell whoever bought him that he wasn't feeling well and feared he might be contagious. He'd explain that he wouldn't be good company and that he'd reimburse them for whatever money they'd spent....

"Three hundred seventy-five!" someone yelled in the back.

"Three seventy-six!" came the response.

"Four hundred!"

"Four hundred and ten dollars!"

Sam tuned out the rising number and tried to smile at a woman in the third row, who was looking at him with what he believed was sympathetic encouragement. She was pretty, with hair the color of Glory's. She even reminded him a bit of Glory, except that she wore studious-looking glasses. She lifted her hand and he thought for a minute she was going to bid, but she tucked a strand of hair behind her ear and offered him a shrug he interpreted as regret.

"Four hundred and sixty dollars. Going once..." The woman at the podium scanned the crowd. "Twice..."

"Forty-seven dollars and fifty-two cents!"

"Sold!" The auctioneer shouted excitedly. "To the young lady at the back for the magnificent sum of forty-seven dollars and fifty-two cents!" The gavel came down and the applause went up and Sam wondered what had happened to his hearing. Forty-seven, fifty-two? But hadn't the bid been four hundred and sixty? And why had everyone in the room reacted with a gasp of astonishment as if the bid had been ten times more?

Several people in the crowd were turning around, looking back to see the lucky bidder. Sam squinted against the spotlight and strained to see the back of the room and just who was coming to claim him.

She marched down the center aisle, her black-patent Mary Janes tap, tap, tapping on the floor. Her red taffeta dress rustled as she walked, and her petticoats extended the ruffled skirt in a crisp circle above her knobby knees. A red bow perched like a butterfly in her wispy blond hair. In one hand she carried a fat, pink, piggy bank and over her arm was draped a dingy, sea green dragon.

"Hi, Daddy," she said when she reached the stage. Then she walked to the podium and proudly handed over the pig. The applause startled her, but Allie recovered quickly and made not one, but three curtsies before Sam picked her up and carried her offstage, followed by the audience's delighted laughter.

"I won you, Daddy!" Allie threw her arms around his neck and squeezed. "I won!"

"You certainly did. Do you think I'm worth all that money?"

"Yes, yes, yes!" She leaned back in his arms to look at him. "You're gonna pay me back, aren't you, Dad? Glory said you would."

"Did Glory arrange this?"

Allie nodded. "It was a mir'cle, Dad. She changed ever'body's mind so we could win ya, even though angels can get in trouble for doing stuff like that, but she said she was doin' it and that was all there was to it. You'll get Mr. Piggy back for me, too, won't ya, Dad? Hunny would miss Mr. Piggy if he didn't come home, wouldn't he, Dad? And guess what, Dad? Glory said we could order pizza tonight! And I get to stay up late and eat it!"

Sam's attention had strayed and his gaze searched through the crowd milling about backstage, looking, hoping, to see one special face. "Where is Glory?"

Allison twisted in his arms to look and then, with a smile, she pointed. "There, Dad. Don't you see her? Right there."

His breath caught in his throat as he saw her, standing alone in the crowd, just inside the dark curtains that separated the stage area from the rest of the room. Dressed in a simple but stunning black dress, with her halo of light hair curling around her face, she reminded him of an Ansel Adams photograph, a perfect contrast of light and dark. She was smiling a secret, special little smile just for him, as if the rest of the bachelors and bidders and support people weren't even there, as if no one else in the world existed. His heart gave a little jump of excitement and, carrying Allie, he threaded his way across the room to reach her.

"We got him, Glory! We got him!" Allison leaned out and wrapped an arm around Glory, pulling her into a three-way hug.

A jolt of electric awareness flashed through Sam as his body came into contact with Glory's. He wondered if she had felt it, too, or if he were imagining a controlled eagerness in the pressure of her hand against his back. His stomach knotted with the desire to be alone with her, to discover how she would react if Allison weren't part of the embrace.

"You got me," he said softly into the hug…and he felt Glory tremble beneath his touch.

"Ow! Don't squeeze so tight, Dad." Oblivious to all but her own desires, Allie wiggled out of the hug to channel her curiosity on the other people in the room. Sam set her feet on the floor and took hold of her hand, but his gaze never strayed from the slight flush in Glory's cheeks. There was a certain hesitancy of movement, a self-consciousness in the way her eyes met his then quickly looked away. He found himself staring at her lips and realized that, despite his better judgment, he wanted to kiss her badly.

Here...now...no matter who might be watching....

"I'm hungry." Allie gave his hand a sharp tug, jerking his thoughts back to reality. "And I want a cheese pizza and a bread stick and a strawberry mall."

"Malt?" Sam suggested the correction as he reached for Glory's hand.

Allie nodded. "Yes, a strawberry mall and Hunny wants—"

"Applesauce," Sam and Glory said together, their fingers firmly entwined.

"With chocolate syrup." Allie patted the dragon's droopy head. "Cause it's a special 'casion."

Sam agreed. "This is the first time I can remember being worth anyone's life savings."

"You're actually worth more than forty-seven dollars and fifty-two cents," Glory said. "But it cost all the quarters we had to park."

Sam didn't dwell on the thought of Glory behind the wheel. And he didn't want to know how she'd managed to top a four hundred and sixty dollar bid with Mr. Piggy's forty-seven, fifty-two, minus a handful of quarters. So he just smiled and said, "It's the thought that counts."

"SHE'S ASLEEP," Glory said as she reached for another slice of pizza. She and Sam were sitting on the living room floor, separated by the coffee table, a Pizza Papa's box, a bowl streaked with dried applesauce, a jar of gooey chocolate topping, a ragged lemon wedge, three crumpled paper towels, a glass one-quarter full of cranberry juice, and a pair of crystal candlesticks that held two half-spent, lighted tapers. "You can check on her again if you want, but she's out for the night."

Sam set his glass on the table. "What makes you think I was about to go upstairs and check on Allison?"

"Weren't you?"

"Lucky guess."

She smiled. "Ethel and the Murkles are asleep, too."

"Believe me, checking on them is the furthest thing from my mind."

"The cat is outside... in case you were wondering."

"I try not to think about the animals in this house." He picked up a stray pepperoni and popped it into his mouth. "Or how they got here."

"I sometimes forget how dull your life was before I took a hand in it." Glory took a bite of pizza and had to use her tongue to catch the stringy cheese and pull it into her mouth. One strand attached itself to her chin and she laughed as she tried to get it off without using her fingers.

He watched, fascinated by her intensity and the concentrated delight she took in each and every mouthful. "You remind me of a chipmunk," he said.

She wiped her mouth and chin with a paper towel. "Simon, Theodore, or Alvin?"

"You've been spending too much time with Allison."

"Impossible."

"No, it isn't. Allie is delightful, but demanding, and you should have some time for yourself." He paused, realizing all of a sudden that she hadn't taken a day off since her arrival. "You're not supposed to work seven days a week," he said, doing some rapid calculations in his head. "My contract with the nanny service specifies that you have to be off duty a minimum of twenty-four hours each week. But you haven't taken any time off at all, have you?"

She shook her head and nibbled at the pizza. "Guardian angels can't take time off. Think what could happen if we did."

"What could happen? Parents might have to curtail their own activities to supervise their own kids while the nannies of the world take a day off? You make it sound like a catastrophe."

"A couple of weeks ago, you would have been the first one to yell catastrophe."

He acknowledged the truth of that with a shrug. "I've learned a few things."

"So have I."

Her eyes met his for a moment, evoking a soft, persistent yearning in the vicinity of his heart. He wanted to kiss her—the desire wouldn't leave him alone, it kept infringing upon his thoughts, thrusting the image into his mind and urging him to act. Now. Before the opportunity was lost.

He began to rearrange the clutter on the coffee table instead. "Why did you come to the auction tonight, Glory?"

"No special reason. Allie just wanted..." Glory stopped on a sigh. "I'd prefer to lie about this, but the truth is, I came to the auction because I didn't want you to spend the evening with another woman, and I was willing to do just about anything to make certain you didn't."

Her answer sent a pleasurable thrill spinning through him, but he tried not to let it show. "I wasn't going to ask, but what *did* you have to do to top the high bid with only forty-seven dollars and fifty-two cents? Bribe the auctioneer?"

She looked offended. "I wouldn't know how to bribe an auctioneer if someone gave me written instructions."

"You'd do it the same way you bribe Allie into doing her chores. You offer a reward."

"Like the satisfaction of accomplishing a task?"

"More like promising pizza or ice cream."

"You mean, I could have just given that woman some ice cream?"

He smiled. "Nothing is that easy, Glory."

"I'm finding that out."

He closed the pizza box and tapped his finger against the lid. "So if you and Allison didn't offer any bribes, how did the two of you manage to walk away winners?"

She developed a sudden interest in one of the burning candles. "Are you sure you want to know? It wasn't very professional of me."

"I like the sound of this already," he said. "Let's hear it."

"Well, in laymen's terms, I guess you'd say I did a little, uh, collective thought intervention."

He mulled over the concept, wondering why he was ever surprised by the words that came out of her mouth. He cleared his throat of an annoying inclination to laugh and tried to match her serious expression. "Collective thought intervention," he repeated. "Are you saying you *hypnotized* everyone in the ballroom?"

"Not exactly," she said, looking a tad embarrassed. "I just sort of gave everyone the idea that the bid was forty-seven *hundred* dollars...and fifty-two cents."

Sam stared at her and then he burst out laughing. "That's rich, Glory."

"It is?"

"No wonder Allison adores you. You're probably the only adult she's ever met who has a better imagination than she does."

"You don't believe me," Glory said with a sigh.

"If you'd wanted me to believe you, I don't think you would have forgotten to hypnotize me."

"Maybe you weren't paying attention."

"But everyone else was? I don't think so." He shook his head in wry amusement. "Oh, I believe you did something to rig the bidding, all right, but you have to admit that *collective thought intervention* is a little hard to swallow.''

''I'm beginning to think you wouldn't swallow a miracle if I wrapped it in mozzarella cheese and offered it to you on a pepperoni pizza.''

''I'm not sure I believe in miracles, Glory.'' He studied the way the flickering candlelight caressed her face and reflected off her curls like a halo. ''Although, lately, with you, I admit there's a certain temptation...''

Her gaze flew to his and her mouth parted in a tiny ''o'' of surprise. ''I'm a temptation?''

''Practically irresistible.''

''Practically.'' She rolled the word on her tongue as if she were looking for a loophole. ''That would mean I'm *not* irresistible. Or I *am* resistible. So I guess that means I'm really not much of a temptation.''

A shiver of awareness slipped beneath his skin as he met her candid gaze. ''From where I'm sitting, you look like the shiniest apple in the Garden of Eden. I have to keep reminding myself of all the trouble that one apple caused.''

''It was just an ordinary apple, Sam. The trouble came from a different source entirely.''

For a long moment he considered the truth of that and tried to recall at least one of the reasons he had for avoiding the very situation he was now in. She was here to care for Allison, not him. And once he crossed the line, yielded to temptation, the trouble would begin. Glory was too innocent of spirit for a liaison between consenting adults, and he was too emotionally scarred for anything more. Temptation and trouble, he thought, and decided he could not have one without the other. He shifted from a sitting position onto his knees, leaning ever so slightly toward her. "Glory, I know where this is leading, but I don't believe you understand what the conseque—"

"Wait a minute." A spark of annoyance flashed in her eyes as she shifted onto her knees to face him across the coffee table. She wiped her fingers on a wadded paper towel, then tossed it on top of the pizza box, and put her hands on the table for support. "You want to know what I understand, Sam?"

"I have a feeling you're about to tell me."

"No, I'm about to show you." She leaned toward him with clear purpose, her lips puckered and ready.

He pressed his hands against her shoulders to keep her at bay. "Let's not start something we can't finish."

"But we can finish! I tried to tell you that before. Sex is one of the in-body experiences I'm allowed to—"

"I don't want to be an *experience* for you, Glory. I want..." He swallowed a sudden, painful knot of emotion. "It has to be more than that. Much more."

"Like what you shared with Jenny?" She leaned toward him and didn't back down when his expression turned defensive.

"Nothing will ever be like it was with Jenny," he said sharply. "Nothing."

"You're right, Sam. So are you rejecting me because I'm not her? Or are you rejecting me because you're afraid I'll leave you like she did?"

For a moment the air was thick with tension as two pairs of eyes clashed and held, as two pairs of lips drew inescapably closer and closer and closer....

Trust me, Sam. Believe in me.

Her words echoed in his head, as clear as a summer morning, her invitation as transparent as a spider's web. And she was right, damn it. He was afraid. Afraid to try love a second time. Afraid to risk the pain of losing someone so precious. Afraid to grow past the point at which Jenny had left him.

Slowly, inexplicably drawn to her, he reached across the coffee table and cupped her face in his hands. He defied her ragged breathing and denied his own strong desire to hold her like that, memorizing the shape of her face, the blue of her eyes, the sweet, tempting curves of her mouth, feeding the anticipation inside him and watching its reflection in the slightly nervous, but anxious parting of her lips.

She wasn't Jenny. Sam wasn't quite sure who Glory was or what she was doing in his life, but his heart accepted her like a familiar melody, absorbing her ready warmth, her unlikely fascination with him, the vast amount of love that surrounded her... and engulfed him in its sensual spell. She might be the puzzle he couldn't solve, a promise he was afraid to claim. But somehow, in ways he didn't entirely understand, he knew he needed her strength to defeat the futile, aching loneliness in his heart.

Bending his head, Sam crushed her lips under his.

Chapter Ten

Like a drowning man, Sam claimed his salvation in a soul-searing kiss. He gathered her against him, indifferent to the hard edge of the coffee table cutting across his thighs, oblivious to everything except the fire in his heart and the heat in his loins. When he felt Glory pull back, he fought her resistance, unwilling to release her, the moment, or the sweet taste of temptation on his lips.

But she was persistent, then insistent, and finally she gasped and jerked away. "Sam," she said breathlessly. "I'm on fire."

He bent his head, intent on recapturing her mouth. "I know. So am I."

"No. I'm on *fire!*" She began flapping her arm and slapping at her sleeve where the candle flame had scorched the sleeve of her dress and set the fabric ablaze.

The smell of smoke was a sobering bite of reality and Sam sprang instantly into action. Pushing the coffee table out of the way, he threw Glory to the floor, grabbed frantically at the edges of the decorative rug, and wrapped them over her until she was cocooned in the smothering folds. Then, shoving furniture out of the way as he moved across the room, he rolled her over and over like an oversize tamale. And when she stopped rolling, he threw himself on top of her and rubbed her carpeted arms to extinguish any lingering embers.

"Sam?"

Her voice was muffled, but sounded blessedly unhurt, and his relief escaped in a long, trembling sigh. "Are you all right?"

"I'm suffocating. Let me out of here."

He shifted his weight and pulled back a flap of the rug until he could see her face. "Is the fire completely out?"

"Believe me, any surviving sparks deserve every bit of oxygen they get."

"You're pretty mouthy for a human torch. Are you in pain?"

"Just this stuffy sort of tickle in my throat. I think I'm...about...to...snee-eezzze—ahh-ahhh-ahhhh..."

Sam flipped the rug over her face in time to muffle her explosive, "Aaaachhhooooo!"

He pulled back the rug flap. "Gesundheit."

Her frown was worth a thousand words.

He unwrapped her like a Christmas present and she lay with her arms straight at her sides, staring at him with wide blue eyes, while her hair formed an aura of static electricity around her head. Laughter caught him by surprise, providing a distraction for his anxiety, a release for his tension.

"Your bedside manner needs work, Sam," Glory said dryly.

He stopped laughing. "I'm sorry. It isn't funny. And I'll bet that arm's really starting to hurt, isn't it? You probably ought to see a doctor."

"The arm is fine and I don't need a doctor. Angels are highly resistant to flames. I just forgot I was wearing clothes." Lifting her arm, she examined the charred fabric of her sleeve. "Good thing the dress is black. Otherwise, this would be really noticeable."

He touched the ivory sheen of her skin inside the blistered opening. It was cool, smooth, and unblemished. "Your skin isn't even red. There's not a mark on it."

"Of course, there isn't. The fire didn't touch me."

Her answer was simple, honest, and completely mystifying. He touched the arm, again. "But I saw the flames... and there's a hole as big as my fist in the sleeve... How could the fabric burn and not..."

She reached up and slipped her arms around his neck. "If I told you, you wouldn't believe me."

"Don't try to tell me this is one of your *miracles*."

"If you don't want to know, Sam, don't ask."

She was right. He didn't want to know. The last thing he wanted to hear right now was another nonsensical explanation. In fact, the only thing he did want was to finish what they'd started. But the interruption was undoubtedly an omen, a warning to be ignored at his own peril.

There was a steady pressure at the back of his neck as she compelled him to come closer, but with some difficulty, he resisted. "We'd better check the rest of the study," he said. "Make sure there aren't any sparks smoldering somewhere in the room."

She wouldn't release him. "Trust me on this, Sam. Nothing else in this room is going to catch fire... except you."

His throat went dry and his heart jabbed against his rib cage like a prize-fighter. For someone who thought of sex as an experience she ought to try, Glory was mastering the moves with incredible speed. And he was fast losing control of his... vehicle.

Relax. Her fingers began a sensual massage at his nape, exerting a slight pressure to draw him closer.

Let go. Seduction called to him in her eyes. Her lips parted in gentle appeal... and Sam decided to surrender. Why should he keep fighting for her innocence, when she was fighting so hard to lose it?

Kiss me.

He obliged, descending on her lips like a sweet, warm rain... and Glory very nearly drowned in the physical sensations that sliced through her body like a spring flood. She gladly would have drowned if that had been the price of the experience. Kissing was pleasurable beyond her most imaginative expectations, but the yearning her lips now shared with Sam's was a desperate, greedy hunger, a need more powerful than she could have foreseen. It was becoming perfectly obvious that her human sexuality instructor had missed a few very important points.

Sam's hand moved against her hair as he smoothed a thick fold in the rug, flattening the wrinkle beneath her head and, in the process, shifting the position of his body against hers. Like a kaleidoscope of colors, the sensations within her shifted, as well. New pressures brought different perceptions and she couldn't help slipping deeper into the feelings, losing her identity in the humanity she had discovered.

Trailing her fingertips past his shoulders, Glory massaged the tension in his muscled back, absorbed the heat of his skin, warmed herself on the flames of his passion. When he took her bottom lip in his mouth and gently suckled it, she gasped and that breathless sensation tightened throughout her body from head to toe. She closed her eyes to focus on the stirrings within her body, concentrating on every nuance of physical feeling.

When Sam used his tongue to create truly intoxicating patterns on her lips, her chin, her neck, her throat, she had to wonder if this body she inhabited could last the night. Night? She wasn't sure it would last another minute. Maybe that's why physical bodies wore out after only a few decades. Maybe they become frazzled under the strain of so much intense pleasure.

He placed his hand on her breast and her pulse flared like a nova. More sensation. More intensity.

More delight. And miraculously, her human heart withstood the frantic assault on its rhythm. How could a mass of muscle and nerve, blood and bone interpret such a physical act and endow it with such deeply spiritual feelings? But it was true. Glory recognized the need to be one with the universe, and yet at the same time she wanted—no, yearned—to belong to just this one man. It was more exciting than she'd expected, more beautiful than she'd thought it was possible to feel. It was as close to Heaven as she had ever been....

Sam was bewitched. The response of her mouth to his, the brush of her hair across his fingertips, the feel of her breast beneath his hand, soft and stroking against him, the slight undulation of her hips—everything about her held him mesmerized. She had enticed him with her laughter, trapped him in her innocence, reminded him of a happiness he'd thought was lost to him.

Glory represented energy and life in a way he couldn't explain. She was all the myriad pleasures he'd ever experienced, every special moment he'd known in his lifetime. She was not Jenny, but for the first time he understood that Jenny was forever gone and that he could close the door of memory to open the window of discovery.

With a reluctance that was as strong as the need to hold on to her, Sam pulled back. He stared down at the flushed cheeks and the rosy bloom of passion on her lips—lips that were so sweet, so tenderly responsive to his—and he wondered if he had plunged in where angels feared to tread. "This isn't a very comfortable position," he said.

A smile began in her eyes and trailed a slow, pleased path to her lips. "You mean there's a better one?"

He drew the backs of his fingers across her cheek, loving the satiny feel of her skin. "Dozens more. Would you rather go upstairs to the bedroom?"

"No," she answered quickly. "If I give you any excuse to get up, I'm afraid you'll change your mind."

"I think you've already given me reason enough to get up and . . . stay up." He smoothed the hair at her temple. "I'm not going to change my mind."

Her lips curved with a sigh. "That's good, because as terribly human as this must sound, I think I'd die of longing if you did."

Heady pleasure stepped up his heartbeat and tingled beneath his skin. He lowered his head to meet the upturned invitation of her mouth, to find again that bewitching softness of her lips. A low groan escaped his throat as the passion took root and flowered within him.

She wound her arms around him and anticipation skittered like mercury through his veins. Her breath was sweetly warm where it mingled with his and he savored the feel, the smell, the taste of her. He'd thought it would feel odd and uncomfortable to hold any woman after the easy familiarity he'd known with Jenny. But Glory proved it wasn't odd in the least, and the only discomfort he felt was the hardwood floor beneath the too thin pad of the rug.

She touched him in a way Jenny never had. The realization was frightening and freeing.

Glory knew it would be easy to forget her reason for being here in Sam's arms at this moment in his life. She knew, too, how deceptively simple it would be at this moment to turn her back on Heaven and stay forever with this man. Now, suddenly, she knew the dimensions of temptation...and they were all contained in a man named Sam Oliver.

Her physical heart raced so fast she didn't understand why it didn't stop dead within her. But a fire raged through her veins, burning her skin, searing her spirit. An angel could die of sensations, she realized. The danger hadn't been overstated. It was as real as the man she held against her pounding heart, as threatening as the thought of the power she now wielded over him, however unintentionally.

And yet, that was not as frightening for her as the knowledge that she was under his power in a way she'd never known before. She was spirit—the blended energy of love and faith, a reflection of the best parts of the universe. But suddenly, in this alien experience of the physical world, she had choices and a vast array of consequences. She couldn't stay in Sam's arms forever. She couldn't even stay in his world much longer. For the first time since creation, she knew the weight of responsibility and the burden of making the right choice.

Sam accepted her touch and responded with an earthy, eager passion. At this moment in his life he needed her physical presence, the body she merely inhabited. The miracle, though, was that she could be present to see, to feel, to taste, to smell, to hear, and to experience this wondrous, mysterious, miraculous blending of their bodies.

His hand on her leg was hot and created an ache deep within her. She moved because it seemed natural to want the silky sensations to continue their sensual upward spiral. As his mouth moved down her neck in a series of moist, heart-stopping caresses, Glory traced his jaw with the palm of her hand. She gasped when his tongue traced the neckline of her dress.

Delicious, she thought. How could anything feel more delicious than the quicksilver shivers that were even now skimming across her skin? His hand slipped beneath the fabric of her dress to close over her naked breast, and she quickly learned that the shivers had only been warming her up for the main event. Lightning impulses flashed through her nerve points and pooled in a sentient ache deep within her. She didn't know what she was supposed to do, didn't know if he wanted her to rub his chest as he was now rubbing hers or just lie still so as not to interfere with his movements. She compromised, cupping her hand over his heart, and waited for his reaction.

It began as a purling sound in his throat and traveled inward. She could feel his pulse increase with excitement, could feel the tightening of his muscles. And somehow—she thought he must have some sort of special powers—their clothes came apart and were discarded. First hers, then his, and then . . . bare bliss.

Glory had thought the physical senses had reached their zenith, but with the first full-length experience of skin against skin, male desire fitting to female acceptance, she knew she'd been wrong. Boy, had she ever been wrong.

His hands became tools of exquisite torture, his lips moved over her body leaving her skin moist and hot and aching for his touch. She was a mass of trembling sensations and she moved her legs, her hips, her arms, her hands in frantic efforts to alleviate the building pressure of her desire.

When at last she felt him push against her, she pooled all her love for him into this perfect blending of bodies, hearts, and souls. She felt complete, whole, happy, and utterly human. And when the passion caught and whirled them into a starry night of seductive kisses and sensual caress, Glory discovered a new way to fly.

"Sam," she whispered softly some time later. "Kissing just got moved into second place as my most favorite experience."

"So far?"

"Ever." She sighed with satisfaction. "And in my case, ever is a very long time."

"DADDY?"

Sam opened his eyes to the disconcerting, beady black stare of a lop-eared dragon. Allie stood beside the bed, holding the stuffed toy so close to Sam's face that he could smell the aged applesauce crusted around the dragon's mouth. He blinked and cleared his throat of husky sleep. "What is it, Allie?"

"Hunny's sick, Daddy," she whispered. "And I don't feel good, too."

Sam raised up on an elbow. "What's wrong?"

A flush rouged her cheeks and tears glistened in her brown eyes as she shook her head, spiking her straight silky hair into straw wisps around her face.

Sick? Sam forced himself more fully awake. "Are you going to throw up?" It was the first and worst possibility that popped into his head. "Is your stomach upset?"

"I don't know. Can we get in bed with you?"

Bed. Last night. Glory. Quickly, Sam pushed one foot back, searching beneath the covers. He knew Glory had been in bed with him for part of the night, but his foot encountered only cool sheets and not a trace of body heat. She wasn't in the bed now, at any rate, and, despite the fact that he would not have wanted his impressionable daughter to find him in such a compromising position, he recognized his disappointment that Glory wasn't beside him.

"Are you hot, Allie?" He placed his hand on her forehead, worried over the misery in her eyes. "Do you need some medicine?"

She nodded without enthusiasm, then turned and walked listlessly into the bathroom, dragging the dragon behind her. Sam made sure she couldn't see him before he tossed aside the covers, grabbed his trousers and pulled them on. As he adjusted the waistband of his slacks, he suddenly remembered the time Jenny's dad had caught him, minus his pants, climbing through the window of her bedroom. He smiled now at the memory, even though it hadn't seemed funny before. Odd that he and Jenny had never laughed about it together. Odder still that he should have the impulse to share the embarrassing details with Glory. She would laugh, he knew. And he would laugh with her....

He listened for a minute to the quiet house, wondering where she was and what she was doing. The desire, the insistent need to see her, was compelling, but Allison needed him and she took priority over everything else. He padded to the door of the bathroom and looked in.

She was asleep on the floor, one arm pillowing her head, the other wrapped around her dragon. She must be sick, Sam decided as worry skeined through his daydreams. He knew so little about how to handle this kind of thing. Jenny had always done the doctoring, medicating, bandaging, and deciding when to seek medical attention. Sam wished he'd been more attentive then, so he'd know now whether to rush Allison to the hospital or just put her in bed and let her sleep.

Stooping down, he brushed the back of his hand across her forehead and down her cheek. She was warm to the touch, but not burning hot. And she wasn't throwing up. That had to be a good sign. He decided to ask Glory for her opinion and, with that thought in mind, he lifted Allie and carried her to the bed.

After arranging the covers around her, he decided she might be too hot under the layers and stripped them off again. But she curled her body around the shapeless dragon as if she were seeking warmth, so he compromised and tucked the sheet over her shoulders. She sighed in her sleep and Sam's heart all but shattered in an effort to hold all his love for her.

Downstairs, he found Glory in the kitchen and stopped in the doorway to watch her. She had her back to him as she fussed with something on the stove, and she was wearing his tuxedo shirt, with the sleeves pushed up to her elbows and the tails clipping her bare thighs just below the hips. Whatever melody she was humming had her moving to the beat, and every few seconds she wiggled her whole body in a sexy little shimmy.

Delight and desire purled into a warm, wondrous feeling that interfered with his breathing and meddled with the rhythm of his pulse. Sam didn't recognize the emotion and wondered if he might be falling in love. The idea seemed unacceptable, somehow, and an odd discomfort tightened around his heart.

At that moment Glory glanced over her shoulder and saw him. She turned, her smile rising like the evening star until it found a home in her eyes. "Sam."

That was all she said. Just his name, in a morning-soft voice, husky with pleasure. But it was enough.

One heartbeat and he was gathering her into his arms. Two, and he was holding her. Three, and his mouth was fastened on hers in a thorough and tantalizing kiss. The world stopped in those few moments, grew hushed and reverent and respectful, and Sam could have sworn he heard Heaven sigh.

When he lifted his head, Glory looked up at him with starry eyes. "I have to tell you, Sam, your kisses curl my toes, but they have slipped to second place on my list of favorite experiences."

"I believe you mentioned that last night."

"Did I? Hmm." She drew her fingertip along his jaw. "I wasn't sure you'd remember."

He kissed the tip of her nose in tender reprimand. "Don't give me that old line. I remember every little detail about last night. Ask me anything."

"Okay. What was I wearing?"

"Moonlight. Next question?"

"What were you wearing?"

"Nothing but desire." He cupped her hips with his hands and pulled her against him. "And I'm thinking about wearing it again today."

"I'm thinking about wearing your shirt from now on."

"You can't do that, I'm afraid. I'll have to have it back."

"When?"

He considered. "Ten minutes. Maybe less."

"What if I don't want to take it off?"

"Then, I guess I'll have to take it off you, myself."

"Oh, sure, you're a big talker now, but you'll get involved in your work and forget all about this shirt and who's wearing it."

"I wouldn't count on that if I were you." He smiled. She smiled back...and his heart got caught in the crossfire.

I love you.

The words were in his mind, on his tongue, poised on his lips, but he couldn't bring himself to say them...not now, not here in Jenny's kitchen. But he wanted to say something to let her know how special she was to him. "There's no way on earth I could ever forget you, Glory."

The smile faded in her eyes, but she hid it by going up on tiptoe to press a fleeting thank-you on his lips. *I'll remember long enough for both of us.* She sent the words to him, but didn't wait to see if he received them. Instead she made a neat turn in his arms and waved her hand at the mess displayed on the countertop. "I've been fixing breakfast for an hour now and the eggs still don't look right."

"The eggs look raw," Sam said over her shoulder.

"I don't know what's wrong with this thing." She picked up the hair dryer and pointed it at the skillet. "I thought you said blowing hot air over food would make it cook faster."

"I was talking about the oven, Glory. The convection oven." His voice was low, stilted, and she felt the vibrations of his humor at her back.

But there was an unfamiliar ache in the pit of her stomach, and she didn't feel much like laughing at her mistake. So she set the dryer on the counter, picked up the skillet, and dumped the eggs into the sink. "Here, you fix the eggs." Turning, she whopped the edge of the skillet against his taut stomach, causing him to give a short "Ooof!" of surprise. Which, oddly, made her feel better. "I'm an angel," she said. "Not a cook." Ducking under his arm, she headed for the door.

"Glory..." He caught her hand, stopping her. Then he pulled her back toward him. "If I embarrassed you, I apologize. It's just that... you have such an unusual way of looking at things."

"Oh, yeah? Well, I'm looking at you, Sam, and what I see is... is... scrambled eggs!" She jerked her hand away and settled it on her hip, not sure if she was experiencing embarrassment or anger, or a post-traumatic sexual frustration—if there was such a thing.

His lips twitched and she decided that if he laughed, she was going to zap him.

"Daddy!" Allison's petulant yell was barely even muffled by the distance it had to travel from upstairs.

"Allie..." Instantly his expression changed, his attention shifted, and his voice thickened with tension. "Damn it, I forgot about Allie. I got so involved with you, I... she's sick and her incompetent father forgets all about her."

"You thought she was asleep, Sam." But he was already on his way upstairs, and Glory knew he was in no mood for reassurance. Especially not from her.

With a sigh, she walked over to the gate that barred the Murkles from leaving their nursery and knelt in front of it. She stuck her arm through one of the lattice-weave openings and, within seconds, the puppies were all over her hand, licking and rubbing, making their sweet little puppy noises. "She was asleep, you know," Glory told them. "Sam's a good father. He has no reason to be angry with himself." Or with her.

But she knew he was.

As she stroked each of the pups in turn, her spirit reached out and upward for her own kind...and met only empty air. No angels were about. Even Leonard didn't answer. Glory added another emotion to her growing list of experiences—although she distinctly remembered one of her instructors saying that angels could never truly comprehend the concept of loneliness.

A few minutes later Sam appeared in the doorway, holding a flushed and clingy Allison in his arms.

"Hi, Glory," she said in a pathetic little whisper as she pulled up her shirt. "Look, I'm spotted."

Glory rose to inspect the red dots on Allie's tummy. She offered Sam a smile, but he ignored the gesture and her intended comfort as he shifted Allie onto his hip and turned away. "I'm taking her to the doctor," he said. "We'll be back."

"When you come home, we'll play connect the dots," Glory said.

Allison's giggle was weak and Sam's response nonexistent . . . unless one counted the succinct closing of the front door behind him.

"I'M BACK, GLORY."

Allison was feeling much better, although her forehead was furrowed in a grumpy frown that signaled all was not well. She flopped poor Hunny onto the kitchen table and climbed onto a chair. Once settled, she propped her chin on her fists and let out a martyred sigh. "I got chicken pucks," she informed Glory solemnly. "And I'm not even a chicken."

Glory looked from Allie to Sam. "Chicken pucks?"

"Pox." Sam set a bottle of medicine by the sink and wadded up the pharmacy sack. "It's chicken *pox*. A common childhood illness which, as I've already explained to Allie, has nothing to do with chickens. Dr. Cooper said she'd be contagious for the next couple of days as the rash develops, but after that she should start feeling better."

"And no one can play with me 'cause I'm 'tagious." Allie's frown drooped even farther into her fists. "I can't play with no buddy. Not even Hunny, 'cause he could catch chicken pucks, too."

"I'm sure that dragons are immune to children's and chicken's diseases," Glory said. "I think it's safe to play with him."

But who'll fix my breakfast? And who's gonna read *The Best Nest* to me and Hunny?" Her eyes got shiny with worried tears. "And who'll tuck us into bed?

And what if I have a bad dream? And what if I can't—?"

"Allie," Sam said. "You're not going to be alone. Glory and I will be here . . . just like always."

"But I'm 'tagious, Dad."

"Only to someone who hasn't had chicken pox. I had it when I was about your age. And Glory probably had it when she was a little girl, so you don't have to worry about being left by yourself. Glory will take care of you while I'm at work, and I'll tuck you into bed at night just like I always do."

Glory tapped him on the arm. "I've never had chicken pox."

He turned. "Please tell me you're joking."

"You know I can't lie about it, Sam. You'll have to be the one to take care of Allie."

"This is the worst time for me to be away from the office. If I'm not there this week, Morrison is going to pull the rug right out from under me on this hospice project. And I can't say that I'll blame him. If I hadn't taken so much time off already..." He jerked open the silverware drawer and took out a spoon, all the while sorting and resorting the problem in his mind. "I'll just have to get someone else to take care of Allie, that's all. I'll hire another nanny."

"I don't want another nanny," Allie said irritably. "If you can't take care of me and Glory can't take care of me, I'll do it myself."

Sam inhaled sharply, reminding himself that she didn't feel well, that she was a bit short-tempered, too.

"Be reasonable, Allie. It'll just be for a few days, until you're not contagious, anymore."

"I'll do it." Glory took a verbal step between father and daughter. "There's a good chance I won't catch the disease and, if I do...well, being sick is something maybe I'm supposed to experience."

"I'll take care of her," Sam said. "I'll just have to work here at the house, that's all." With that settled, however unsatisfactorily, he picked up the medicine and carried it to the table, then carefully poured the cherry red syrup onto the spoon. "You're supposed to take two doses of this every four hours, Allie. Open up."

She looked at him, lips pressed shut.

Glory stepped closer to help and Sam caught the movement from the corner of his eye. "Get out of here, Glory," he said. "And for the next few days, stay out of whatever room Allie is in...unless you want to experience chicken pox. They say adults have a rougher time with it than kids do." He held out the spoonful of medicine. "Open your mouth, Allison."

She refused with a shake of her head, and Sam frowned. From the doorway, Glory could see this escalating into a real battle of wills, which wasn't going to make anyone feel any better. Inspiration struck like a magic wand, and she tucked her hands in her armpits and flapped her arms like a chicken.

Allie mimicked her action and went her one better...opening her mouth to crow, "Cock-a-doodle-doo!"

And that's when Sam popped the spoon into her open mouth.

"DID YOU HEAR SOMETHING?" Sam sat up in bed and Glory pulled him back down beside her.

"You're imagining things," she said. "If you want out of this bed, all you have to do is . . ." She demonstrated and he moaned.

"Will you stop that? I thought I heard Allie calling me."

"She's asleep, Sam. The medicine makes her sleepy."

He turned his head to look at her, mesmerized by the way the moonlight in the bedroom transformed her hair into a halo around her face, shocked anew by the intense serenity of the love that seemed to be everywhere in the room, in the whole house, in him. "Maybe I should try giving you a dose of that medicine so I can get some sleep."

"You can sleep later." Her hands caressed him, fondled and aroused him. "Haven't you ever heard the saying 'make hay while the sun shines'?"

"The sun set hours ago, Glory."

She nibbled at his ear. "Pretend, Sam. Close your eyes and pretend."

He closed his eyes . . . and the sun began to rise.

Chapter Eleven

Mitch Morrison hated cats. So the moment he took a
seat in Sam's study, Dobbin jumped onto his lap.

It was not an auspicious beginning.

"Would you mind getting rid of this?" Morrison
picked up the cat by the scruff of the neck, leaving no
doubt about what "this" he wanted to be rid of.

Sam took Dobbin and smoothed his ruffled fur before putting him outside in the rose garden and closing the French doors. It was a nice day with a pleasant
breeze and the study would be stuffy with the doors
closed, but that was the only way Sam knew to keep
the cat out. He heard a scratching sound as he turned
to his guest and hoped the darn cat wasn't going to
spend the next thirty minutes clawing at the door.

Morrison shifted his considerable weight in the
chair. "I never figured you for a cat lover, Sam."

Sam eyed the big chair behind the desk, but in the
interest of keeping this unexpected visit informal, he
chose to sit next to Morrison in front of the desk.

"The cat was a stray and my daughter got attached to it, so it stayed. You know how kids are."

Morrison nodded, but it was obvious he had his own agenda, and small talk wasn't on it. "Let me get right to the point. I've pledged a great deal of financial support for this hospice project of yours and I've convinced some of my friends to pledge their support, as well. My name is out there on the line on this, you understand."

"I'm deeply appreciative of all you've done, sir," Sam said with sincerity, even though he knew Morrison expected the words of gratitude for his generosity and influence.

"I know you are, Sam, but here's my problem. A year ago, when you first broached the hospice idea, I was hesitant about buying the old hospital building. But I respected your reputation and I had no cause to doubt your professional judgment on the building's condition. I'll be the first to admit I was swayed by your enthusiasm and passion for this project. A man wanting to help others as a tribute to his wife's memory is a powerful inspiration."

Morrison leaned forward in the chair, comfortably ensconced in Sam's territory. "But lately I've had second thoughts about your commitment...and I don't like second thoughts, Sam. Especially not when my friends have been very generous based on my recommendation. To my knowledge, you haven't made the trip to Seattle to look at the renovation of a similar building, much less prepared a detailed report so the city can process the required permits. In short, we're no further along than we were when we acquired the old hospital building. Now, I realize you spent a lot of time overseas last year, but you assured me this project wouldn't suffer from neglect and that when you returned to Tulsa, you'd be ready to begin work in earnest."

Sam nodded, maintaining the appearance of being riveted on Morrison's every word, even as he tried to pinpoint the source of a slight scratching noise that kept preempting his attention.

Morrison settled back in his chair, smiling benignly, like a father who after scolding his son is willing to impart forgiveness. "I don't have to tell you, Sam, that what has happened is the further deterioration of the building and an increase in the cost of repair and renovation. My friends are calling. They want to know what's wrong. And that's what I'm asking you, Sam. What in *hell* is going on?"

"Ommmmm. You're not supposed to say that word." Allison popped up from behind the desk, a limp dragon draped over her shoulder, a plump brown-and-white bundle of wiggling puppy under her arm. "Children and puppies aren't supposed to hear 'dults say bad words like that 'cause then they might say the words to get 'tention. See?" She came around the desk, holding out the puppy. "See what big ears he has? He couldn't help hearing the bad word you said. And now he'll say it and Ethel will be mad and—"

"Allison." Sam stood, half-afraid Morrison would reach out and grab her by the scruff of the neck. "What are you doing in here?"

"Hi, Daddy," she said with a wide, happy smile. "Me and Murkle Two are havin' a meetin'. Just like you, Dad."

It was a calculated comment, packed with all the bright-eyed adoration she could throw in for good measure...and Sam was ashamed to admit that it worked like a charm. "You're not supposed to be in here, Allie. Why don't you—"

"You want to see my puppy, don't ya, Mr. Moresun?" She advanced on Morrison with a tidal wave of stalling tactics. "Isn't he cute? His name is Murkle Two. You can pet him if you're real, real, real careful. Don't be afraid, he doesn't bite hard." She thrust the pup onto Morrison's lap and leaned on the stiff arm of his chair while she swung her feet back and forth like a pendulum. "Have you had the chicken pucks, Mr. Moresun? I have. See?" She lifted her bangs to show off the numerous, but fading, marks on her face. "And now Glory has them. And she's grumpy. Are you grumpy? You sound grumpy when you open your mouth. Do you have a kid like me? What's her name? Does she have a puppy?" Allie laughed. "Look! He's tryin' to lick your shirt."

Morrison lifted the puppy in one beefy hand and dropped it a short distance to the floor. The puppy yelped, but Allie yelped louder and her eyes flashed.

"You meanie! Beat him up, Dad. He hurt Murkle Two."

"The pup isn't hurt." Morrison turned an expectant frown on Sam and it wasn't hard to figure out what was wanted. As if Sam would pick up his daughter and put her outside with the cat. Sam realized that he didn't like Mitch Morrison. He hadn't asked for this meeting, didn't believe he needed to defend himself, and there was no excuse for dropping the puppy, even if it wasn't hurt.

"Let's continue this meeting another time, Morrison," he said. "I'll call you and set up an appointment."

"But aren't ya gonna beat him up, Dad?"

"No, Allie. I don't beat up people." He leveled a caustic gaze on Morrison. "Or puppies."

Morrison rose unhurriedly and with an air of superior amusement. "I suppose I can hardly complain about being asked to leave when I did drop in without calling first. But I'm going to tell you, Sam, that I dropped by unexpectedly for a reason, and your little angel here has given me the answer."

"Glory's an angel, and if I ask her to, she'll zap you!" Allie made the threat from the safety zone behind Sam's legs, and Morrison laughed.

"You're a spunky little thing, aren't you?" he said.

Allison bared her teeth and growled like a bear.

Reaching back, Sam put his hand on top of her head to silence the outburst. Obviously her bout with chicken pox had wiped out every last bit of manners

Jenny had taught her. But he'd be damned if he was going to scold her in front of Mean Mitch Morrison. "My office would be a better location for our next meeting," he said. "I'll ask my secretary to set up a mutually agreeable time."

"Don't bother. As I recall, your daughter managed to interrupt our meeting at your office, as well. I'd hoped you would have hired someone capable of taking care of her by this time, but it's obvious your priorities have changed and you're no longer totally committed to the hospice project. I'm going to call in another architect, Sam . . . someone with fewer family responsibilities."

Sam felt like Morrison had ripped him into two pieces. The hospice was his plan to commemorate Jenny's life, a lasting tribute to her memory. But he had to think of Allison. And it was patently obvious that Morrison didn't believe he could do both.

"I'd like the opportunity to discuss this at another time, Mr. Morrison. I'm still as committed to the project as ever. But I also have an obligation to my daughter."

"Yes, of course, you do," Morrison agreed. "Just as you have an obligation to the people who invested in you and your project."

"There's a difference, Morrison, and you know it."

With a nod, Morrison walked to the door. "No one ever said life's choices were easy, Sam. I'll see myself out. Goodbye, young lady. Take good care of your pup."

He had no sooner left the room than Allie came out fighting and would have tackled him like a fullback if Sam hadn't held her back. "Settle down, Allie. He didn't hurt the pup."

"I'm tellin' Glory. She'll zap him!"

"Glory doesn't zap people. Not even when she's sick." The thought of Glory was soothing, even if she had been a little testy lately. Just the idea that she was nearby eased his agitation. Glory had become his sounding board, his best friend, his most trusted advisor, his lover...

That pleasant line of thought had just become tantalizing when he heard the jangle of the bell he'd so ill-advisedly given her when she'd first gotten sick. "Sounds like she wants to see us," he said, even though he didn't know why she had to keep ringing and ringing and ringing the damn thing. "Let's go see what she needs."

"IT ITCHES," Glory said. "And it isn't very nice of you to laugh, Leonard. This chicken pox experience was your idea, not mine."

She sat on the padded window seat and settled her back—carefully—against the wall, drawing her knees up and resting her hands in her lap, staring at the blotches and blisters on her skin. "Tell me this, Leonard, did you have to have a childhood disease during *your* in-body experience? Uh-huh. That's just what I thought. If you had any idea how much I want to scratch..."

Shifting position, she tried not to think about her discomfort. "Of course I know the reason. 'Illness is a part of the human experience and angels should understand the pain factor.' But this isn't pain, Leonard, this is a nuisance. And what good is it to anyone in this household? I can't be with Sam. He can't leave the house. He's frustrated with all the responsibility of taking care of Allie and of me.... What do you mean, he needs to be needed?"

She frowned out the window at the perfect day. "Well, that isn't much of an explanation. And I don't feel very *angelic* right now, thank you. You're my supervisor, you're supposed to know when I need help, not just pop in and out whenever you feel like... What? Now, that is not true. I talk to you all the time, you're never around to hear me, that's all."

But he was right. She knew it all the way to the bottom of her angel heart. She was the one ignoring the truth, ignoring him. He wasn't around to hear her because she no longer wanted him around. She wanted to be in this body, in this house, in Sam's life. And with every moment that passed, her wants were becoming her reality.

In the big oak tree outside the window, she noticed a pair of robins coaxing their baby out of the nest, forcing it to make that first frightening attempt to fly. In the yard below, Dobbin lay in wait, tail twitching, eyes on the baby bird that fluttered to the ground within easy reach. Glory glared at the cat...but nothing happened. She blinked in surprise and tried again. Dobbin crouched lower, ready to spring, un-aware of—and unaffected by—her effort to inter-vene.

Then suddenly, Dobbin jumped straight up, as if he'd been struck by lightning. He hit the ground on all fours and bolted up the oak, clawing his way higher and higher to the top of the tree. The robins hovered over their baby, urging it to fly.

Thanks, Leonard.

You have wings, Glory. Fly....

She heard him call to her in leaving, but she didn't answer. Instead she picked up the bell Sam had given her and rang it as hard as she could.

"HIGHER, SAM. You'll have to climb higher."

Sam clung to a limb of the old oak and frowned over at his cheering section, Glory and Allison, who were leaning out the bedroom window. "Climb higher," he muttered. Easy for them to say. He ad-justed his hold on the rough bark and looked up through the branches, trying to spot the cat he was supposed to rescue.

"Dobbin's cryin', Dad. He wants to come down."

"That makes two of us," Sam said under his breath as he inched his way up to the next branch. Stupid cat. Why had he climbed the tree in the first place if he couldn't get down? Why had Glory been looking out the window at that particular moment, anyway? And why had he let her persuade him to be the hero?

"Come here, kitty," he called, and got a whiny "Meow" in return. With a frown, Sam eyed the branch a foot above him and then reached up to grab it.

He missed and slid back, scraping his arms, chest, and stomach, tearing a hole in his shirt, and bruising his already aching ego.

"Watch out, Sam!"

"Be careful, Daddy!"

They were certainly quick with admonitions and encouragement, he thought. Almost as quick as they were demanding. Why else was he in this tree? Why else had he spent the better part of the past two weeks taking care of them? And neglecting work that was intensely important? Morrison was right. He had welshed on his promises regarding the hospice. And that was only one of a dozen projects he'd shuffled to the back burner to stay home. Wasn't that the whole purpose of having a nanny? So he could work with the assurance that his child was supervised and cared for? How had it happened that Glory seemed to take nearly as much care as Allison?

In a burst of frustration, Sam swung up to the next branch and grabbed the cat. The sound of enthusiastic clapping burst through the spring green leaves just as Dobbin dug his claws into Sam's hand, took a gigantic leap, and clambered down the tree in a quick— and independent—retreat.

"Oh, poor kitty. Is he all right?"

"Did you hurt him, Daddy?"

That was it, he decided. Enough was enough, and he had had enough. He was an architect, damn it. And it was time he went back to acting like one.

No matter what the women in his life might have to say about it....

"I'M GOING TO SEATTLE on business," Sam announced over dinner.

Allison stopped building a pyramid with her carrots to look at him. Glory laid down her fork.

"I have an early morning flight tomorrow," he continued in his best this-is-no-big-deal voice. "And I'll be back Thursday."

Glory didn't say anything, but he could see the questions welling up in her eyes.

"We'll have to take Ethel and the Murkles, Dad." Allie warmed to her own interpretation of the plan. "And Dobbin and Hunny. And I'll take *The Best Nest* so we can read and—"

"Allie, this is a business trip. I can't take you or the animals with me. You remember about business trips, don't you?" Considering his numerous and lengthy trips to Europe last year, it was probably the worst thing he could have said, and Sam made the connection a second too late. "I'll be back almost before you know I'm gone."

"No!" Allie dropped her spoon on her plate, sending a carrot soaring across the table. "You can't go away. Not without me and Glory. Hunny will be real mad if you leave him behind."

"Don't start, Allie. I have to go. It's important." Sam turned his head to look at Glory, but she didn't offer a word of support.

Allie picked up the dragon and held his scraggly chin so he could stare at Sam, too. "Hunny wants to go, Dad."

"I am going on business and you are staying home."

"But I don't want to stay home."

"Well, you are. That's the way it is and there will be no further discussion."

"That's not fair." Allison pouted.

"You might have given us a little warning, Sam," Glory said, quietly adding fuel to the fire.

"I don't have to be fair and I didn't know about the trip until just a little while ago."

"But you must have known the trip was coming up. You could have—"

"I could have, but I didn't." Sam did not see any logical reason to feel guilty about this. It was a two-day trip, for heaven's sake. "Here's the deal. I'm going. You're not. Period. I'll drive myself to the airport in the morning, and I will see you both Thursday evening. Now, can we please finish our dinner?"

"I don't want this stupid dinner!" Allie's eyes filled with angry tears as she slid off the chair seat. "Hunny *hates* carrots!"

Sam glimpsed the insecurity in her eyes and his heart broke for the worry he'd unintentionally added. In a rush of understanding, he reached for her and tried to gather her into his arms for reassurance, but she jerked away and stared at him as if he'd suddenly betrayed her secrets to the enemy.

"I'm only going to be gone for two days," he tried to explain. "You and Glory will have fun by yourselves. You can play with the puppies and with Ethel and Dobbin. You can watch television and read books. You can even invite one of your little friends over. And before you know it, I'll be back. I'm not going away forever, Allie."

"I want you to go away," Allie said. "And I don't want you to come back forever! Do you hear me? Don't come back!" With Hunny clamped tightly in her arms, she stalked from the room with her chin pointed so high in the air it was amazing she could see where she was going.

Sam watched her stomp up the stairs and decided that when he got back he was going to introduce structure and discipline into his daughter's life. She was becoming completely unmanageable. In many ways, Glory had turned out to be more permissive than Allie's grandmother. He turned an accusing look on the only other person left to share the blame.

Glory answered with a shrug. "I think she's upset."

"Really? Then that makes it unanimous."

"I'm not upset, Sam. I just don't want you to go."

"Why not? Are you afraid the cat might climb another tree and you won't be able to get it down? Or are you worried about getting attacked by another household appliance? Or maybe you just don't want to handle Allie all by yourself? Is that it, Glory? Are you so dependent on me, you're afraid to be left on your own?"

Annoyance and hurt flashed at him from her eyes. "There's no need to attack me, Sam. I'm not the one who said I hoped you never came back."

The hurt settled in him, heavy and helpless. "She didn't mean it. She's just too young to understand."

"She's afraid."

"Everyone's afraid. She should get used to it."

Glory traced a circle on the table with her fingertip, but she didn't know what to say, how to tell him that fear was like a perpetual thief, stealing the daily treasures from his life.

"What about you, Glory? What are you afraid of?"

She kept on tracing the circle, following the unbroken line around and around. "Time," she said finally. "I'm afraid of running out of time. It's funny, isn't it? Time is just a concept. I never gave it a thought, never even perceived its passing. And then I meet you and I start counting every single second..."

His fingers touched her chin, warm and insistent, and she had no choice but to raise her gaze to meet his. There was wonder in his midnight eyes. And hope. And when he leaned slowly across the table toward her, still holding her chin with the slight pressure of his fingertips, she took his hope and gave it a home in her heart. He claimed her lips in a fragile and irresistible kiss that left her empty with need and aching with desire. Her hands clung to his shoulders and she felt the inexplicable sting of tears. "Sam," she said against his lips, "I want to be with you every moment. I want to enjoy the time we have together."

He trailed kisses to her temple and nuzzled her curls with his mouth. "I have to go on this trip, Glory. Don't ask me not to go."

"Don't go, please. Stay here with me."

Her hair ruffled beneath his sigh. "You're beginning to sound like Allison. Are you getting ready to stomp your foot and tell me not to come back forever?"

"I would never tell you that, and you know I have a very tenuous contract with these feet. If I stomped one of them, I'd probably end up flat on the floor."

"You may end up on the floor, anyway." He began to nuzzle her ear, sending delicate shivers cascading through her. "And I may end up there with you."

She let the sweet surprise of his touch filter into an achy sensation inside her. "Do people have sex in the kitchen?"

"I don't know, Glory, but it has suddenly become an appealing prospect."

"Who peels first? You or me?"

His laughter caressed her with desire even as he established a measure of distance between them. "Don't tempt me. We'd have to clear the table and find some way to lock Allie in her room and... It's a delicious thought, but I think we'd better save it for a more accommodating time."

Glory could feel her time with Sam slipping away and she made a grab, thinking she would hang on to as much of it as she could. "Would that be nine or eleven?"

"Nine players on a baseball team, eleven for football," he said with a grin. "What are we playing, Jeopardy?"

"Indoor sports," she replied smoothly. "You be skins, I'll be shirts. That way we know which team we're on."

"Obviously, you haven't played this game enough. Otherwise, you'd know that we both have to be skins. Matching outfits only allowed in the bedroom."

"Or the kitchen?"

"Aprons only."

"What if the apron sash gets caught in the blender?"

"We won't turn on any appliances . . . just one another." He leaned in and crushed any further nonsense on her lips, spreading the warm, intimate taste of his pleasure.

Don't go, Sam. Stay. Stay with me. . . .

But she knew he didn't hear. Her power to slip thoughts into his mind had given way to the human power her body had over his.

And Glory decided it was not a bad trade.

"Sssshhhh, Hunny!" Allison put her finger to her lips before she opened her bedroom door. It made the tiniest squeak and she froze, standing as still and quiet as a mouse, waiting to see if anyone had heard. When the house stayed silent and dark, she tiptoed into the hall and eased the door shut behind her, flinching as the latch clicked into place. There was no sound from the far end of the hall, so she took a deep breath and held on to it as she picked up her going-to-Grandma's suitcase and tiptoed down the stairs.

Chapter Twelve

With his hand on the doorknob, Sam paused outside Allie's bedroom and argued with his guilty conscience. He'd be a complete idiot if he opened this door. But what kind of dad would leave without saying goodbye?

A cowardly dad, that's what kind.

He could live with that. Especially when he considered the scene that was sure to ensue if he woke her up to tell her he was leaving. He'd compromise with his conscience and call home during his layover in Dallas. He'd talk to Allie then and promise to bring her a T-shirt or a stuffed animal or.... Who was he kidding? He'd bring back *whatever* she wanted.

Cowardice, compromise, and bribery. With those tenets of parenthood firmly in mind, he picked up his suitcase and started down the stairs. Jenny would be ashamed of him, he thought. She, certainly, would never have allowed Allison to get so out of hand. Then again, if she hadn't been so efficient, he wouldn't be having this trouble with their daughter now.

It felt good to blame Jenny for a change, and he redirected his guilt at her all the way to the kitchen. He heard Ethel snuffle a good morning at him from the laundry room, but he resisted the stupid impulse to give her a pat on the head before he left. Rousing the Murkles would be nearly as bad as waking Allie, so he didn't even speak as he passed through the kitchen to the back door and quietly let himself out. He'd grab a bite of breakfast at the airport and, thereby, avoid even the remote chance of another confrontation with his daughter.

Glory didn't even cross his mind until he was backing the car out of the driveway. Which seemed odd at the very least. Of course, he'd told her goodbye, promised they'd discuss their future upon his return, kissed her—a few times—and said he'd see her Thursday. But considering that he thought he was in love with her, it was strange that he had gone even five minutes without thinking about her. Wasn't it?

He'd been with Jenny so long, he wasn't sure he knew what falling in love felt like. Damon said love was the most fun a man could have while suffering a severe case of heartburn. But then Sam had never looked at love or life as a single man. He'd been one part of a couple for nearly as long as he could recall. And now . . . well, now there was Glory.

Glory, the miracle worker.

Glory, the mysterious.

Glory, the—

Sam reached across and tapped the clock on the dash. Then he switched on the radio and jumped from station to station until he caught the correct time. Glory, the little schemer, he thought as he floored the gas pedal. She had reset all the clocks in the house and he had barely fifteen minutes to make his plane.

Damon was right. Love and indigestion. Two sides of the same coin.

GLORY DISCOVERED the missing Murkle first. She counted the pups again—one, two, three, four—just to be sure, then raced up the stairs to Allison's room, knowing before she opened the door that the child was gone. Her presence wasn't anywhere in the house. Even with her muted abilities, Glory could pick up on that indisputable fact.

So where was Allison?

And why hadn't Glory sensed her distress? How could she not have *known* Allie was going to run away? A mother would have considered the possibility, been on the alert for signs that might signal such an event. But Glory wasn't Allie's mother. She was a guardian angel... and a rotten one at that.

"Sam?" she called, but she knew he wasn't in the house, either. Just her luck that he'd awakened early. In all likelihood, he was already at the airport and running to catch his plane. And if he hadn't stopped to check his luggage, he might just make it, too.

"Luggage," she whispered, seeing in her mind's eye the oversized bag he'd packed last night. "I've been meaning to get something smaller," he'd said. "This was fine for a trip to Europe, but it's a trifle big for an overnight stay in Seattle."

Allison could have fit inside that suitcase—with room to spare. Room enough for a floppy dragon and a fat, little puppy.

But she wouldn't have gotten inside a suitcase. And Sam surely would have noticed the added bulk. And the puppy would have made a noise . . . or an odor. It didn't even bear thinking about. No five-year-old child was going to put themselves in a dark, cramped space, much less zip themselves in. It made more sense to think Allison had simply walked away from the house.

Simply walked away? Panic smacked Glory square in the heart. "Leonard!" she called. "Get down here immediately. Something terrible has—"

Terrible? Are you sure?

"What do you mean, am I sure? Allie's gone. She must have left sometime during the night. I . . . wasn't paying attention. I don't know when she left or where she went or what was in her mind. She was angry with Sam. You have to help me find her, Leonard. Show me where she is, tell me how I can get to her."

You have wings, Glory.

But she didn't. Not anymore.

"I KNOW I MISSED the flight," Sam explained to the perky airline agent at the departure gate. "What I *don't* know is when I can get on another flight."

"Sir, you'll have to take your ticket downstairs to the check-in counter. Someone there will help you."

"Someone *there* sent me back *here* to you."

She batted her perky eyelashes and battened down her perky smile. "But they shouldn't have done that, sir. You'll have to take your ticket—"

"Downstairs to the check-in counter, I know." Sam finished the sentence, picked up his suitcase, and lugged it all the way from the concourse to the escalator and downstairs again. "I missed my flight," he said with admirable calm as he set the suitcase on the dais next to the check-in counter. "I need to be on the next plane to Dallas so I can make my connecting flight to Seatt—"

"Sam!"

He turned and saw Glory motioning frantically to him from halfway across the lobby.

"Sir?" The agent at the check-in reclaimed his attention. "If you'll give me your ticket, I'll see if there's a way for you to make your connection."

Sam looked from the agent back to Glory.

"Ssssam!" she hissed his name again, and with an apologetic shrug for the agent, he handed over his ticket and walked away from the counter. Now what was she doing at the airport? She wasn't wearing a matching outfit today. Just a pair of faded blue jeans, a T-shirt that read, Angels Take Themselves Lightly, and a frazzled look. Her hair, like always, was a riot of sunshine around her face. She wasn't wearing shoes, and even after her prank this morning, his heart rose like a rainbow at the sight of her.

"What are you doing here?" He asked the question even as he slipped his arm around her and pulled her against his chest. He covered her mouth in a long, luxurious kiss and when he lifted his head, he didn't even try to look annoyed. "If this is your idea of a rousing send-off, I'm willing to be persuaded. But it's a good thing you didn't arrive any earlier."

She didn't smile, and for the first time he saw the distress in her eyes. "Oh, Sam," she whispered, and his stomach plunged to his shoes, taking his heart along for the ride.

Allie? He couldn't even mouth her name, couldn't begin to ask the question. Just stood there, dying in giant leaps of dread.

"She's gone, Sam. I looked in her room this morning and she wasn't there. Her overnight case is missing and one of the puppies, too."

He swallowed hard. "Hunny?"

"Gone."

"Where? How could she...? Why would...?" But he knew the why. It was the where he had to focus on. "Did you call the police?"

Glory shook her head. "Leonard."

"You called someone named Leonard?"

"Of course. He's the Apprentice Angel Advisor."

Sam gave her a little shake. "Snap out of it, Glory. The Guardian Angel agency isn't going to be of much use to us now. We'll call the police, tell them to start searching the neighborhood.''

"Leonard said I'd find her here."

"How would he know?"

With a frown of unholy impatience, Glory's gaze swept the area. "He knows these things, Sam. He said I'd find what I was looking for with you. So, she has to be here."

Sam scanned the lobby, trying to make sense of that, trying not to jump from one terrible possibility to another, trying not to hear the dirge that was his heartbeat. "But what would she be doing at the airport? Are you positive you looked everywhere she might have hidden in the house?"

Her grip on his arm pinched. "She's here, Sam. I don't know what she's thinking. I don't know where she is. But I know she is somewhere inside this building. She . . . she has to be."

"There's no way a five-year-old child could get to the airport without an adult to—" He looked out at the street, at the cars moving past. "She's in my car," he said. "That's it. She got in the car and rode here with me. And I never even knew she was back there."

He strode toward the automatic doors.

"Sam—"

"Sir—"

The calls whipped past him like grains of sand in a windstorm. Glory, the ticket agent, his suitcase, the trip to Seattle. . . . None of it touched him. His fierce love for Allison was all he recognized, his fear for her safety was the only thing that kept him from crumbling to the floor in agony.

She would be in the car.

It was the only thought he allowed himself to have.

SHE WASN'T IN THE CAR.

Glory knew the emptiness Sam would find even before she caught up with him in the parking garage. She had enough angel mind left to see the unoccupied place behind the front seat, to sense the warmth of the small body that had been there, but wasn't now. And her heart already ached with the devastation that assailed him when he opened the door and looked inside the car. Her only thought was to comfort him as she placed her hand on his arm.

"Don't touch me," he said in a voice quiet with fury. "That's been the problem all along. You and me...instead of me and Allie. You, wheedling your way into our life with your *miracles*. Well, find the miracle in this!" He gestured at the empty station wagon and the terrifying silence that was pouring out. "Where is she, Glory? What have you done with my daughter?"

Stunned must be the word for this frigid emotion she felt. Stunned and utterly helpless to defend herself. Maybe she was at fault. Maybe somehow, with the best of intentions, she had ruined everything. But how could she have stopped herself from falling in love with Sam? Even with all the warnings she'd had, Glory knew she wouldn't have prevented it if she could. "It's pointless to turn against me, Sam. I'm on your side. If I knew where Allie was, if I had even an idea, you'd know it, too."

"What about that advisor? You talk about him, but I've never seen him. Does he have Allie?"

"He has her best interests at heart."

"Oh, I'll just bet he does. Where is he now, Glory? And where is my daughter?"

"You can't think that Leonard—"

His fingers closed on her upper arm. "I can think it, Glory. My daughter is missing and I am holding you personally responsible if anything happens to her. Do you understand? I'll sue everyone. I'll make sure the Guardian Angel Nanny Service is blown out of business and off the map. And, if any...harm...comes to Allison, I'll blast you and your *angel advisor* off the face of the earth."

Stunned wasn't the word. Shattered was the only thing that came close to describing what she felt as she stared into Sam's embittered eyes. She loved this man, had loved him long before their meeting, and would love him long after their few moments together were gone. In every facet, in every form, body and soul, she was in love. Deeply, desperately, in love.

And she could never have imagined how much it would hurt.

"I love you, Sam," she whispered. "And I love Allison."

"Yes, well, love doesn't mean much to me right now." He released her and slammed the car door. His fear was a terrible, tangible thing, a starving lion seeking sustenance and with sudden, uncompromising, and very human insight, Glory understood that fear, too, was a part of loving.

And she stepped in to be the sacrifice.

"I can find her, Sam, but you'll have to help me."

"No, Glory, I'm not playing your silly game." He turned away, took several steps, and stopped. He put his head in his hands, devastated and immobilized by his terror of losing Allison . . . and Glory felt her heart break all over again.

She's all right, Sam. Trust me. She's all right.

He heard her . . . even though the words had gone straight from her spirit to his. She knew he had received them by the straightening of his shoulders, the lessening of tension that rippled across the muscles in his back. But when he lowered his hands and turned to look at her, she saw the suspicion in his eyes.

Believe in me, Sam. Believe in miracles. Believe in something beyond what you see.

He wanted to fight. She could see that, too, in his eyes. But he couldn't battle on two fronts. Fear and faith each demanded total surrender, and he could choose only one to defend. No matter what he wanted to believe, no matter how difficult it was to let go, he could choose only one.

All right, Glory. I believe. I believe in angels. I believe in you.

His answer flowed into her like the sweet scent of a freshly scrubbed cherub, and she gathered it in with all the joy in her angel's heart. She had chosen Heaven. Sam had chosen life. The world was full of miracles.

Glory closed her eyes and opened her senses, reaching out to embrace Sam with her boundless love, reaching further to carry the combined force of their love to Allie. And like the day at the ice rink, she lived again the wondrous experience of flying.

She's inside the building. Glory sent him a shared vision. *Near something red. She's sharing an ice cream with Hunny and the Murkle. And there's laughter and smiles and people who care.... Look, Sam. Look, everything is all right.*

Sam closed his eyes and took a deep breath as he caught the image. A picture came to mind, as clear as a cloudless sky and just as serene. Allison was sitting on top of a check-in counter, swinging her feet back and forth above several sturdy pieces of luggage and one small, going-to-Grandma's overnight case. Several uniformed airline employees were gathered around her and it was obvious that amusement was not in short supply. Everyone seemed to be laughing, entertained by whatever Allie said. She was holding an ice-cream cone in one hand and was offering alternate licks to the puppy and Hunny. Her hands and face were a sticky orange-colored mess, and the puppy kept lapping his tongue over his dog lips as if he couldn't get enough ice cream flavor.

Allison was safe. She was waiting for him with no thought that he wouldn't come. Glory had arranged this, Sam knew. She had taken his panic, his fear of loss, and transformed it into the promise that the important things in his life were, and would continue to be, all right.

"Are you coming with me?" he asked, and instantly felt her regret.

Kiss her for me.

He paused, the strangest mix of emotions squeezing his heart. "What about me, Glory? Who's going to kiss me?"

Her answer was slow to form and dreamy, like a fading light, but her voice in his mind was still as pure and beautiful as a newborn morning. *Someone special, Sam. Someone very special. Watch for her and trust your heart. It has a graceful way of leading you where you need to be.*

"And you, Glory? What about you?"

I'll be around. Riding herd on a bunch of cherubs, probably. Sweeping up stardust here and there, but never far away. You can't escape from me, Sam. I'm your guardian angel.

"You're a miracle," he said with conviction.

Yes. One miracle in a life brimming over with them.

Sam turned in a slow circle, hearing her laughter, feeling her love, knowing he wouldn't see her again, but needing to take one last look all the same.

He was alone . . . and yet he understood that he had really never been alone at all. And would never be again. He believed in angels. Who would have thought this could happen to him?

The answer came like a promise.
Allison.

"AND THEN, DADDY, the puppy licked my face and I waked up. And then I saw you walkin' away and I yelled, but you kept walkin' faster and faster and I wanted to cry, but I didn't. And then Hunny said we should hurry up and I got the puppy and Hunny and my suitcase and I opened the door and then I closed the door. And then I runned inside and looked ever'-where and then Hunny started to cry and then the puppy started to cry, but I didn't start to cry, Daddy." She leaned back in his arms so she could look him in the eye as he carried her out of the airport terminal and into the parking garage. "Can I go with you to your work, Daddy? I'll be real, real quiet and I promise not to bother you, 'cause I want to stay with you, Daddy, for ever and ever and ever and ever and . . ."

"Allison . . ." Sam shifted her in his arms, along with his grip on both suitcases, the puppy bouncing in his jacket pocket, and the limp dragon hanging across his arm. They were still two rows away from the station wagon, but he was so happy to have Allie safe and sound and chattering like a magpie that he felt like he could carry the whole kit and caboodle all the way to Seattle. "Guess what, Allison?"

"What?"

"I love you."

"Oh, Daaaad! You said that already."

"Can't I say it again?"

"I 'spose. If you want to."

"I want to. I want you to know how important you are to me and how worried I was when I thought you weren't safe and how very happy I was to see you sitting at that ticket counter."

"I was just waitin' on you to find me." She pecked his nose with a kiss. "Hunny was worried that you wouldn't never find us, but I knew you would, 'cause you're the best daddy in the whooooole worrrrllllld." And to prove it, she hugged him again as tightly as she could.

Sam stopped in his tracks and set down the luggage, so he could hug her back. "I will always find you, Allison. And if you're ever afraid or lonely, I want you to just close your eyes and think about how much I love you."

"Do I hafta close my eyes?"

With a shake of his head and a hug from his heart, he tweaked her nose. "No, Allie, you don't have to close your eyes."

"Good, 'cause I might fall asleep and... Dad?"

"Yes?"

"Did Glory go back to Heaven?"

Sam paused, wondering what to say, how to answer what he couldn't understand. "I don't know, Allie. I don't know where Glory is."

Allison patted his chest. "I think, maybe, she's in here. In our heart."

A lump the size of his memories blocked his throat for a moment. *Don't be silly,* Glory had said. *Heaven's much closer than that.*

Sam swallowed hard before he placed his hand over Allison's over his heart. "I think you're right, Allie," was all he could manage to say. "I think you're right."

LOOK AT THEM, *Leonard. Have you ever seen anything more beautiful? They're perfect. Absolutely perfect.*

They're human.

So was I....

You can go back, Glory. Say the word and I'll send you back.

To be something I wasn't created to be? That wouldn't be right. Not for them and not for me. But, oh, I was tempted....

You made the right choice.

I know, but... they won't even remember me, Leonard. Allison will go on believing in angels, but her memories of me will be nothing more than imagination. And Sam won't have any memory of me. For them, it will be as if I was never in their lives, at all.

Love is the footprints you leave behind, Glory. Trust me, it will be enough.

Why didn't you tell me I'd get so attached to them?

Experience is the best instructor.

That's a cop-out, Leonard. I'll bet you didn't know.

I knew. Just as I knew what your choice would be.

Now, how did you know that?

Because you have wings, Glory. And you want everyone to fly. Come along, let me show you your next assignment....

You mean, I'm not reassigned to the cherub corp?

You're an angel first class, Glory. No more riding herd on mischievous cherubs for you.

Hmm. I suppose that means I'll have to create my own mischief. I'm only kidding, Leonard. Let's... Oh, wait. I forgot something. I have to go back. Just for a minute. I have one miracle left to do. It will only take a touch....

Glory...?

Chill, Leonard. It's just one more footprint. For Sam....

Chapter Thirteen

Allison scooted around the corner and raced through the study with the puppies yipping at her heels. She slid to a wide-eyed stop in front of the closed French doors. "Dad, look! It's a mir'cle!"

Sam walked up behind her, ready to tease, wondering if she had inherited any of her penchant for drama from him. "You're right," he said. "I see five Murkles...no, make that six..." His teasing trailed into an astonished silence as he caught a glimpse of the tapestry of color outside. Slowly, he reached past Allie and turned the latch. The doors swung open to a garden reborn in rich hues and heady fragrance. Everywhere he looked were bushes bursting with blooms in every shade of rose against a background of variegated greens.

Allie slipped her small hand into his and Sam's fingers closed tenderly around it. "It's a mir'cle, isn't it, Dad?"

Yesterday the rose garden had been dead, dry and brittle. But today.... He leaned close to smell one of the flowers. The petals were dew-drop fresh, the foliage thick with new growth, the branches supple and resilient with life. "It certainly looks like a miracle, Allie."

"It is, Dad. I know it is."

Sam cupped his hand on her shoulder and they stood in the doorway together, absorbing the mystery, silenced by the wonder. "This is incredible," he said finally.

She looked up at him. "You know what I think, Dad?"

"What is that, Allie?"

"I think we must have a garden angel."

Sam looked down and saw the unwavering faith in her eyes, knew that in her innocence she believed totally in the angels she talked about so often. It was undoubtedly one way she coped with her mother's absence, and who was he to tell her that angels had better things to do? Someone had touched this garden and brought about a miracle. And even if he knew who and why and how at this very minute, Sam knew he couldn't, wouldn't even try, to change Allison's mind. A garden angel was a better explanation than any he could provide.

"Do you think she's still here?" he asked. "Should we look for her?"

"Daaaddd, you're silly. You can't see an angel."

"Why not?"

"'Cause you just can't." She put a hand on her hip and surveyed the garden. "But sometimes they leave footprints."

Sam was impressed that she knew so much about angels, a subject about which he knew only what was in literature . . . and in the storybook Allison loved for him to read to her. *Glory, Angel First Class* it was titled, and he'd read it aloud so many times he knew every word by heart.

The phone rang and Sam winked at Allie before he went inside. "Good morning," he answered, and realized suddenly that it was. It was a miracle of a morning and, with the phone in hand, he walked back to the doorway to enjoy it.

"Sam." Damon's voice held an unwelcome tension. "Morrison just left the office."

Allie went from rosebush to rosebush on hands and knees, pushing back the leaves, digging in the dirt, looking for angel footprints. Sam smiled. "The strangest thing has happened, Damon."

"I know. That's what I'm calling to tell you, Sam. Morrison took the hospice file with him. He said he's taking the project out of your hands, Sam, and giving it to Keith Miller."

"Okay," Sam said into the phone receiver.

"Now, don't panic, I think I know how to . . . Did you just say *okay*?"

Sam chuckled as he watched one of the puppies lick Allie's bare toes. "I was expecting Morrison to do something like that, Damon. And I'm okay with it.

Yesterday morning, maybe I wouldn't have been, but today... I'm okay."

A pregnant pause pumped through the phone line. "Wait a minute, I think I may have dialed the wrong number. Sam, this hospice project is your baby. I've hardly been able to get you to talk about anything else for the last couple of months and now, all of a sudden, it's *okay* for Miller to take over?"

Sam didn't quite understand it himself. "Damon, something unusual has happened."

"You're telling me."

"It's not about the hospice. That doesn't really matter to me anymore. Of course, I'd love to see it completed, I'd love to do the project, but as of yesterday, building a memorial to the past is not on my list of priorities. I have another tribute to Jenny in mind."

Allison rolled on the ground while the Murkles cavorted around her. Puppy barks and little-girl giggles spooled through the study in delicious reels. There was life in Jenny's rose garden and after a long, cold winter, there was once again life in him.

"You really should come over here, Damon," Sam said. "There's something you need to see."

Damon's sigh was long on patience. "I've seen the puppies, Sam. I've seen the cat. I saw the goat before you gave it to the petting zoo. I've seen Allison in person and in pictures and on videotape. There is nothing at your house that I need to see."

"You have to see this garden."

"Give me a break. Wait, don't tell me, you finally dug up all those dead plants and put in a hot tub as I suggested many times."

"You're not going to believe your eyes."

"I'll be right over. Can I bring a date?"

Sam raised his eyebrows. "No, Damon. I'd just as soon Allison didn't meet every woman who skims through your life."

"I never thought I'd say this, but Meredith isn't a...uh, skimmer. She may be around for a while."

"Now I must have the wrong number. Who's Meredith?"

Damon cleared his throat. "'Heaven, Tonight' from the bachelor auction."

A wide grin broke across Sam's lips. "So, Mr. Fantasy Guy finally gets his just deserts, huh? Well, all I can say is, no one deserves it more than you."

"Deserves what?"

"Indigestion."

"Laugh all you want, Sam. Instead of taking a chance on meeting a woman you might actually want to date, you contributed almost five thousand dollars to spend an evening with your daughter."

"It was for a good cause," Sam said, with his eyes on Allie. "So when are you bringing Ms. Tonight by to meet us?"

"Meredith and I will stop by around noon, if that's convenient. We're having lunch together and since you're working at home, we may as well have lunch at your house."

"Allie and I will be waiting. In fact, we're waiting for an applicant from the Guardian Angel Nanny Service right now. I was beginning to think they'd forgotten all about sending someone after Mrs. Maggard left so abruptly. But everything worked out for the best, anyway. Allie and I have had time to adjust and I've been thinking more and more that I may continue to work at home... for another year or so, until she starts first grade."

Damon groaned. "I can't talk about this now," he said. "Someone has to take care of the office, you know."

"I know... and it's a comfort to know it's in capable hands."

"Yeah, well, you owe me."

"Yes, Damon, I do." Sam hung up, set the phone aside, and started to join Allison and the Murkles in the garden, but the doorbell chimed out a few glorious bars of the "Hallelujah Chorus" and he changed direction.

One peek through the foyer window made him frown. The woman on the porch was facing away and all he could see was a long expanse of shapely legs beneath a pair of cut-off jeans and a white T-shirt with some sort of radio station logo on the back. She was barefoot, too. If this was Mrs. Klepperson's idea of a suitable nanny....

Sam opened the door and the woman turned around, only to freeze in surprise. "Sam?" she questioned softly. "Sam Oliver?"

"Yes." He'd never met her before. He was almost certain he hadn't, but there was something familiar.... Sam stopped staring at the sunshine curls that frizzled around her attractive face and forced his gaze to the morose-looking basset hound in her arms.

"Is this your dog?" the woman asked, thrusting Ethel toward him. "I found her in my yard, going through my trash, and I thought she ... well, since it's pretty obvious she has puppies, I figured she probably lived somewhere nearby."

"You live here?" Sam hoped he didn't look as stupid as his question sounded. "I mean, in the neighborhood."

"Around the corner and down maybe half a block. I've just been going house to house." She made a wry face. "I can't bear for animals to be running loose. You never know what could happen to them and I ... Well, I'm glad I found you. I mean, you, her owner. I mean, I'm glad this is where she lives."

Sam took Ethel and felt a lightning bolt of instant attraction when he accidentally touched the blonde's hand. "Thanks." For the life of him, it was the only word he could get out of his dry mouth.

"No problem." She stood there, shifting from foot to foot, as if she couldn't decide whether to stay or go. "You don't remember me, do you?"

With tremendous regret, Sam shook his head. "I don't know how I could have forgotten. You look so ... familiar."

She shrugged. "I have that kind of face, I guess. People are always telling me I remind them of someone. I keep thinking someone will say they recognize my voice." She paused, then explained. "I do a little radio work."

"Radio?" Sam said eagerly. "I listen to the radio."

"Oh, well, I'm only on once in a while. The DJ is a friend and he likes to have me talk about analyzing dreams. It's not really a scientific report or anything, but he says the listeners love the segment."

"Wait a minute. I heard that." Sam didn't think he could have felt more pleased if she'd presented him with a check from the Publishers' Clearinghouse. "A few weeks ago. That was you?"

Her lips pressed in a rueful line as she nodded.

"I'm impressed." Ethel began to squirm, so Sam bent down and put her on the floor. She had nice legs, he thought—the woman, not Ethel. "I don't know anyone with . . ." Legs. He'd almost said "legs." "On radio. With connections on radio, I mean."

"I'm a psychologist in my *real* life, so I suppose that makes it sound more impressive, but anyone who can read could talk about dreams."

Sam stood there, looking at her, feeling possibilities, wondering how to begin. "I must have been dreaming when we met," he said with surprising sincerity. "That's the only excuse I can offer for not remembering."

Her smile was a ray of sunshine and her laugh a little like gold. "We didn't meet. We just made eye contact. At the charity auction."

The memory fell into place. "Third row, fourth seat over?"

"That was me."

"I do remember. I thought you were going to bid, and I was a little sorry I'd already arranged for Allison to win." He stepped back, hesitated, then took the plunge. "Would you like to come in for coffee? We can sit outside in the rose garden, if you want. You can meet Ethel's puppies. And Allie. And...maybe we could talk a little about dreams."

"I'd like that. Thank you." She held his gaze as she stepped inside—and promptly tripped over Ethel.

Sam's reflexes kicked in and he caught her in his arms, but Ethel barked a protest, and in trying to avoid stepping on the dog, he lost his balance and went down, pulling the blonde down on top of him. When he opened his eyes, he found himself staring into eyes as blue as Heaven. "Hi," he said. "I'm Sam."

"I'm happy to meet you, Sam," she said. "My name is...Grace."

For a moment laughter hovered between them, silently building to a shared enjoyment. And when he heard her laugh, Sam knew that somehow, in ways he couldn't begin to explain, his heart had already made her acquaintance.

It was, as Allie said, a mir'cle.

Once in a while, there's a story so special, a story so
unusual, that your pulse races, your blood rushes.
We call this

Borrowed Time is one such book.

Kathleen Welles receives a most unusual offer: to sell one past day in her life for a
million dollars! What she didn't realize was that she'd be transported back in time, to
the very day she'd sold—the day she lost her true love, Zachary Forest. Can she right
her wrongs and reclaim the man she loves in a mere twenty-four hours?

#574 BORROWED TIME
by
Cassie Miles

Available in March, wherever Harlequin books are sold.
Watch for more Heartbeat stories, coming your way soon!

Take 4 bestselling love stories FREE

Plus get a FREE surprise gift!

HARLEQUIN®

A M E R I C A N ✦ R O M A N C E ®
®

He's at home in denim; she's bathed in diamonds...
Her tastes run to peanut butter; his to pâté...
They're bound to be together...

for Richer, for Poorer

We're delighted to bring you more of the kinds of stories you love,
in FOR RICHER, FOR POORER—a miniseries in which lovers
are drawn together by passion...but separated by price!

Next month, look for

#575 RYAN'S BRIDE
Julie Kistler

Don't miss any of the FOR RICHER, FOR POORER
books, coming to you in the months ahead—
only from American Romance!

IS BRINGING
YOU A BABY BOOM!

NEW ARRIVALS

We're expecting! This spring, from March through May, three very special Harlequin American Romance authors invite you to read about three equally special heroines—all of whom are on a nine-month adventure! We expect each soon-to-be mom will find the man of her dreams—and a daddy in the bargain!

So don't miss the first of these titles:

#576 BABY MAKES NINE
by Vivian Leiber
March 1995

Look for the New Arrivals logo—and please help us welcome our new arrivals!

NA-G

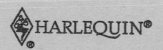

Harlequin invites you to the most
romantic wedding of the season.

Rope the cowboy of your dreams in
Marry Me, Cowboy!

A collection of 4 brand-new stories,
celebrating weddings, written by:

New York Times bestselling author

JANET DAILEY

and favorite authors

Margaret Way
Anne McAllister
Susan Fox

Be sure not to miss Marry Me, Cowboy!
coming this April

 **HARLEQUIN**®

MMC

 HARLEQUIN®

Deceit, betrayal, murder

Join Harlequin's intrepid heroines, India Leigh
and Mary Hadfield, as they ferret out the truth
behind the mysterious goings-on in their
neighborhood. These two women are no milk-
and-water misses. In fact, they thrive on

Watch for their incredible adventures in this
special two-book collection. Available in March,
wherever Harlequin books are sold.

HARLEQUIN®

Don't miss these Harlequin favorites by some of our most
distinguished authors!
And now, you can receive a discount by ordering two or more titles!

HT#25577	WILD LIKE THE WIND by Janice Kaiser	$2.99	☐
HT#25589	THE RETURN OF CAINE O'HALLORAN by JoAnn Ross	$2.99	☐
HP#11626	THE SEDUCTION STAKES by Lindsay Armstrong	$2.99	☐
HP#11647	GIVE A MAN A BAD NAME by Roberta Leigh	$2.99	☐
HR#03293	THE MAN WHO CAME FOR CHRISTMAS by Bethany Campbell	$2.89	☐
HR#03308	RELATIVE VALUES by Jessica Steele	$2.89	☐
SR#70589	CANDY KISSES by Muriel Jensen	$3.50	☐
SR#70598	WEDDING INVITATION by Marisa Carroll	$3.50 U.S. $3.99 CAN.	☐ ☐
HI#22230	CACHE POOR by Margaret St. George	$2.99	☐
HAR#16515	NO ROOM AT THE INN by Linda Randall Wisdom	$3.50	☐
HAR#16520	THE ADVENTURESS by M.J. Rodgers	$3.50	☐
HS#28795	PIECES OF SKY by Marianne Willman	$3.99	☐
HS#28824	A WARRIOR'S WAY by Margaret Moore	$3.99 U.S. $4.50 CAN.	☐ ☐

(limited quantities available on certain titles)

	AMOUNT	$	
DEDUCT:	10% DISCOUNT FOR 2+ BOOKS	$	
ADD:	POSTAGE & HANDLING	$	
	($1.00 for one book, 50¢ for each additional)		
	APPLICABLE TAXES*	$_____	
	<u>TOTAL PAYABLE</u>	$_____	
	(check or money order—please do not send cash)		

To order, complete this form and send it, along with a check or money order for the
total above, payable to Harlequin Books, to: **In the U.S.:** 3010 Walden Avenue,
P.O. Box 9047, Buffalo, NY 14269-9047; **In Canada:** P.O. Box 613, Fort Erie, Ontario,
L2A 5X3.

Name: _____

Address: _____ City: _____

State/Prov.: _____ Zip/Postal Code: _____

*New York residents remit applicable sales taxes.
Canadian residents remit applicable GST and provincial taxes.

HBACK-JM2